A Grammar of Endings

A Grammar of Endings

Alana Wilcox

THE MERCURY PRESS

The publisher gratefully acknowledges the financial assistance of the Canada Council for the Arts and the Ontario Arts Council. The publisher further acknowledges the financial support of the Government of Canada through the Book Publishing Industry Development Program (BPIDP) for our publishing activities.

Canadä

Edited by Beverley Daurio
Author photograph by Lorne Bridgman
Composition and page design by TASK
Printed and bound in Canada
Printed on acid-free paper

1 2 3 4 5 04 03 02 01 00

Canadian Cataloguing in Publication Data
Wilcox, Alana
A grammar of endings : a novel
ISBN 1-55128-086-8
I. Title.
PS8595.I53167G72 2000 C813'.6 C00-932201-9
PR9199.3.W476G72 2000

The Mercury Press
www.themercurypress.com

anomia [G. *a-* priv. + *onoma*, name]. Nominal *aphasia.* Inability to access the names of things, people, or places in the mental lexicon although they are subjectively perceived.

"That's what they mean by the womb of time: the agony and despair of spreading bones, the hard girdle in which lie the outraged entrails of events."

— William Faulkner, *As I Lay Dying*

"Writing: a way of leaving no space for death, of pushing back forgetfulness, of never letting oneself be surprised by the abyss. Of never becoming resigned, consoled; never turning over in bed to face the wall as if nothing had happened; as if nothing could happen."

— Hélène Cixous, "Coming to Writing"

abiosis [G. a- priv. + *bios*, life]. **1.** Nonviability. **2.** Absence of life. **3.** Abiotrophy.

I summon them through my stillness, ask them to come to me, brisk, furtive green. I wait between the steel bed and this cotton blankness, this white sheet my last letter to you. A bright light overhead to illuminate its clear grammar, the starkness of its metaphor. Intently now, they come to me, footfalls loud as gunshots in this last dance, clean hands sheathed in rubber. A jury of stainless steel. Deep voices brushing the microphone: my final kiss. They pull back the sheet, fold it carefully.

The absent stethoscope. Knives so sharp; I lie naked on this cold table and they enter me, these blades, with a lick. Residual tenderness in their hands, as though I might yet bruise, as though my blood still might be summoned to the surface. I imagine their touch to be yours, my sweet Aidan, and my legs part slightly into their hands. Longing for you through this stillness, that I might hold you while you read this letter. Against the clumsiness of your hands I imagine precision, careful lines drawn across your body with a scalpel; a layer of your skin removed in one clean sheet. To excise your love for me this way, to receive, at last, a letter from you. (An epidermal love.)

They skim my breasts, cold damp rubber like an unwelcome dawn, and prise apart my chest. They make me offer myself to them as I did to you. Tugging at my organs, palpating, admiring their resilience. Powers of divination, they imagine an end for me. Organs scattered like tea leaves. A cloying belief in the possibility of closure. Traces of gunpowder tunnelled through the roof of my mouth. Sharp lines written up my forearms. Smudged bruises, ropeburn around my throat. Shreds of skin under my nails. Or, quieter: whispers of sleeping pills in the lab work, insomnia of the blood. The kiss of a plastic bag deep into my open mouth. My narrative lost to the coldness.

Their droning voices, such long words. My body a stream of syllables; it is a foreign tongue to me, the words crumble into dark meaninglessness. I hear only the sounds that are in your name, constellations of phonemes barely legible in a black sky. A vision of your body luminescent before me, lunar; the crescent of your hip pressing into my thigh.

They reassemble my body like a clock.

& & &

My dearest Aidan,

I ache for you. My breaths shallow, my heartbeat irregular, shying from your voice through my veins. Shoulders atrophied, crumpled, my body tries to close itself around the last of your

Night presses in against me like water. Desire, circling. Words sinking beneath my reach. There is no room for reconsideration, the page too dim for revision. Each word heavy with the hope that it will be enough. The dull impossibility of such a letter. I toss the wadded paper across the room to silence its glare. Should I acquiesce to your silence.

My dearest Aidan,

I ache for you, the way you might hold me, how night holds its darkness pressed so tightly to itself against the threat of dawn

Ache: such longing in this word, the only one that might be enough. Onomatopoeic almost, the sustained *A*, rent suddenly, *K*. But I crumple this page, too. Rhyming, *ache* and *fake* and *take*, these resonances never far away. *Break, quake*. Such darkness crowding in under my pen, I cannot see my words, the shapes that might redeem them; the way the *C* and *H* kern, huddle in together, inscribing a tiny circle, a sanctuary.

My dearest Aidan,

& & &

I would love you like a book. Symmetrical, unpredictable. Pages pressed flat together, words deep and fleshy through the thickness. Letters immutable and sequential; I would love you with the certainty of the other side of the leaf. Indelible as ink. Irrevocable as binding, as reading. The strictness of page numbers, the gentle sound of a page turning. I would assemble the indices of every book ever written and bind them together and this would be my letter to you.

& & &

If only I could shape Aidan into words, then he would be extricable. But on paper he is only more present.

I thought I saw him on the street yesterday. The same red hair, square jaw, unforgiving gait. And even though I knew it wasn't him, my blood rushed away from my heart. This happens so often; my imaginings of his presence accumulating and solidifying until one day it really will be my Aidan.

Sometimes what I want to say is so clear, so lucid, I can fit it into a single sentence. But by the time I reach the period, the beginning has evaporated because nothing is large enough to accommodate this. And then I can't remember what colour shoes he had when we met or what the first movie was that we saw together. It makes me desperate with fear, this failure of memory. Over and over I play back to myself the story of the first time we made love until it becomes banal; I try to touch my breast the way he used to, but I can't remember. I can't recall what he looked like naked. I try to remember the pattern of red hair on his chest, but then I wonder if I'm thinking of a photograph of someone else. I try to mimic the feel of his hand, possessive and reverent around my waist, but I forget to account for the prescience of loss.

I want not to care about these things any more, I want simply to write this letter and be done with it. I want these memories to fall, spinning gracefully, until they land, a soft shroud on the earth, like leaves, like snow.

abulia [G. *a*- priv. + *boule,* will]. Aboulia; loss or impairment of the ability to perform voluntary actions or to make decisions.

The language of you, the equivocal grammar of you, my Aidan. Lingual; the sentence of you.

To parse you, to conjugate this love. I lie on your bed at the beginning of this, some subject. The verb of you.

To love, always transitive. The myth of completion, of symmetry around the verb.

Words of you. How you catch in my throat, falter. Love, arbitrary as any grouping of letters, elusive as the perfect sentence. I speak you over and over, as if I might shape the words into the meanings I have for them. The finality of the period; how I might end every sentence with a colon:

Out of breath, bereft:

& & &

> My love has made me selfish. I cannot exist without you. I am forgetful of every thing but seeing you again— my Life seems to stop there— I see no further. You have absorb'd me. I have a sensation at the present moment as though I was dissolving— I should be exquisitely miserable without the hope of soon seeing you.
>
> John Keats to Fanny Brawne

& & &

You lead me into the shower, cold porcelain against my skin, and you sweep your tongue across my body, weaving a web around me, and the water obscures my face, runs down my throat, I swallow again and again. I climb over you around you and you push so deep into me I think there can be no room left for any of me. Wet, you inside me, and I feel my body bruising against the hard porcelain. You pound into me your teeth ripping at my breasts until they swell deeper into your mouth your fingers digging under my hipbones as if to spread me wider until I can take your entire body inside me.

Until our skin is raw, our pores opened to each other in testament to our nearness. We move to the bed, you fall asleep still inside me on top of me around me and it feels like only one of us has to breathe, only one of our hearts has to beat. I am quaking from the inside out and I am crying and I am alone in my own bed and I am choking on the smell of you.

& & &

Once, with trepidation, my father took us fishing. I endured the precariousness of the boat, the quiet, the anguish of the small fish. And then, when it was dead, I watched with envy as my father gutted it, the knife sharp and certain through its body, as if the steel might bisect history.

(To eviscerate our love this way, without hesitation. To cut clean through to the marrow of grief.)

& & &

A slow peace through my body when I arrive at the library. A repository of quiet facts, an infinitude of knowledge. Words coy between bindings.

Like every morning, I am alone until eleven. There is a tranquillity to these solitary rituals, the low thud of books as I stack them. I can almost hear my pulse, ricocheting off the metal shelves. *(Ai-dan)*. No. I drop a book a little too heavily, begin sorting and piling too vehemently, the rhythm erratic. I can keep you out of here, the books on the shelves pressed so tightly together, a rainbow of spines to keep your face away, the cushion of millions of pages to absorb the sound of your voice.

You were inside here only a few times, early to pick me up. How incongruous you were, scuffed black shoes against the short beige carpet, red hair bright, unruly, beside the monochrome of the computer screen. Your clothes meticulously dishevelled. Old jeans held to your meagre hips by a wide belt. A faded black t-shirt, leather jacket. Leaning warily against the beige metal shelves, shifting uncomfortably away from the bright books, their impervious bindings, their transience. I so seldom look to this image— you, frail, inside my sanctuary.

acataphasia [G. *a-* priv. + *kataphasis*, affirmation].
Inability to correctly formulate a statement.

My father, lurking among these words to Aidan. As though I could map the place where two losses intersect, as though there were some secret language to be found in that chiasma, some code that has been eluding me that would be *enough*. I am voracious for words about my father. I imagine conversations I might have with him, but I never believe them; I can never remember the sound of his voice, the patterns of his speech. Only gestures, the way he moved his hands as he spoke. The shape of his toenails. A visual memory, an auditory amnesia.

So I savour the words around him. The stories others tell, the books he read, the words of his death. For this last, I have borrowed a medical dictionary from work; sometimes I can find him there. How beautiful, the language of disease. It has a cipher, certain groups of letters that always refer to the same things. *bio* life *neuro* nerve *cardi* heart. And *a*. Negation, deprivation, absence. A prefix added to take something away.

I have been reading, from the beginning of the dictionary, about diseases. From *A*. I am afraid of *H*, an *A* fallen, lax. That final place of my father. So I go slowly, moving through the body with each disease, feeling each death as it might enter, through the liver, the foot, the colon, the heart. I can feel its spectre there, in every place; the ways in which the body might disintegrate.

& & &

> A love letter by its very nature has to be an intensely personal communication from one person to the other... The chief topic and, indeed, the whole purpose of the letter is to bridge the gap between the two people, or to express through the written word what it is difficult to put in the spoken word. It is always fitting to emphasize in a love letter the burden that the separation is putting on the writer and to state how the other person is always in the writer's thoughts... Writers of love letters should say what they have been doing while apart from the loved one—without, of course, appearing to have been enjoying things too much on their own.
>
> Nigel Rees, *Letter Writing*

& & &

Work has become tedious. Shelve the books, retrieve the books, stamp the books; I feel such loathing for them. The concise language of call numbers. The unequivocal finality of black on white, mocking my attempts to write this. Sometimes I slam them on the cart too hard, as if to jostle their words, disturb the order of the letters, their complacency. And then I catch myself and I am ashamed. Especially today, because someone noticed. A strange man, *Ethan,* he said. He has been here often lately, so I was particularly embarrassed that he saw me slam the book down. He looked up from his work, startled, and smiled. I blushed, tried to pretend that the book had slipped, but I was certain he knew I was simply frustrated, being always in the midst of such beauty, such perfection, a constant reminder of my own incompleteness, my own failures of articulation.

& & &

> Aware of you, chaotically. I love this strange, treacherous softness of you which always turns to hatred... I didn't want love because it is chaos, and it makes the mind vacillate like wind-blown lanterns. I wanted to be very strong before you, to be *against* you— you love so to be against things. I love to be *for* things. You make caricatures.

> It takes great hate to make caricatures. I elect, I love— the welling of love stifles me at night—

Anaïs Nin to Henry Miller. So lucidly incoherent. I have been reading the love letters of others, looking for us in their lines. But they are hardly more adept than I am at encapsulating love between salutations. *for— against.* This is a beginning, but it cannot explain to you that time when in the middle of making love I began crying and hitting at your chest. *foragainst, lovehate, happysad, moreless, notenoughtoomuch.* There is not space enough in these dichotomies for the vicissitudes of love; there is not room enough in love for the coexistence of these extremes. How to accommodate chaos between *dear* and *yours truly*. Evelyn Waugh to Laura Herbert: *I love you more than I can find words to tell you.*

& & &

The refusal of my body to acquiesce to linearity; how then can I ask my language to adhere to an order. Limbs unruly, not sequential but centrifugal. Words of you like this, awkward, connected only by their proximity to you. Haphazard, tangled.

And when I sit down to write to you, language unravels itself. Some words of you vanish, leaving only the haunting certainty of their prior existence, of their loss. Phantom limbs. Others are present, but deadened, numb, and I can wield them only bluntly. Verbs decay into adjectives, nouns deflate into prepositions. Until there is only an amputated vocabulary, a grammar of chaos. Anchorless, without the weight of meaning.

& & &

I would love you in the sky. Doubt brief as birds, the respite of clouds. The persistence of blue. Dawn, slow and sure as meaning; how the sunlight forces itself through the clouds, diffuse and intrepid as desire.

& & &

Your absence, unbearable. My heart too empty for sleep or wakefulness. An insufferable stillness in

Too naked. Plain words cannot convey the wake of chaos you have left in me. The ugliness of their nudity— cellulite hips, distended abdomens, thick, fleshy arms. I am afraid of their awful simplicity. Perhaps they will seduce you better if you have to undress them. Perhaps I can better tolerate their tyranny if it is cloaked in robes of fiction.

Once upon a time there was a beautiful princess who had been awakened from a slumber of one hundred years by a charming prince. They were married in the grandest celebration the kingdom had ever seen and lived very happily. But the princess could not shrug off the fear that the prince did not love her. She knew that if she had happened upon a beautiful stranger in the woods, she would not hesitate to steal an insignificant kiss, unaware that it might carry the weight of permanence. The princess would hide herself away to consider this in a corner of the grounds where they had forgotten to clear away the vines and brambles of the hundred-year sleep, and this thought would grow, lush and dense as weeds, until she could imagine that while the prince was off hunting in the forest he would happen upon another beautiful sleeping princess and her own life would be undone. He did not notice her sadness, busy as he was, and it grew and grew until it was almost as thick as slumber

Inadequate. There is no genre wide enough for the fairy tale of love; no story slow enough to accommodate the enormity of fingers brushing against a thigh, no story fast enough for the rushing of blood through the veins. There is no place for linearity in the soft curves of love, and treachery.

Perhaps the expansiveness of metaphor; an extended conceit to articulate myself.

My heart a cauldron, you

Tactless.

The acrid smell of faith in the air; morning riding in through the silence. Rays of sunlight easing themselves between the bars and into my cell. My last sunrise. I hear them stacking the wood and I wonder if I will find the smell of you in the smoke, if I will find the softness of your tongue in the lick of the flames. What sorcery you have committed. You have made us believe the witchcraft was mine. Your velvet spells, your prophecies of rapture. Your incantations, my name over and over until the word melts into a moan, the pattern of your lips moving a devil's genuflection.

The rope binding my hands tickles the backs of my thighs, taunts. Slivers in my fingers from digging at the post behind me. Tendrils of smoke rising up between my toes into a caricature of our bodies pressed together. Flames yearning towards me the way I reached for you. I will rise above myself and watch this effigy burning. I will float over the jeering crowd and I will breathe my hot smoky breath down onto you until you are hard with the heat, until you sweat blood.

A coven of sorrows.

I lift the letter into the candle.

acathexis [G. *a*- priv. + *kathexis*, retention]. A mental disorder in which certain objects or ideas fail to arouse an emotional response in the individual.

Morning, when the lie of the body is silenced. Desire a foreign tongue in the glare.

I step in front of my mirror, examine the thigh, how the trace of your handprint has been stretched and distorted. You would not recognize yourself there. I run my hands up and down my sides again and again, harder and harder. When the flesh resists, I rake my fingernails up my stomach. I am pleased with the suddenness of red written there. (My letter.)

:you bewitched me with words:

I run my hands up and down my body again, tracing the red marks with a soft finger, and I try to remember the way I would do this before I could imagine you might love me. My fingers harsh and callused now, they were so gentle then, I would imagine it was you touching me, my eyes just open enough to see the colour of your hair. So very red, almost the colour of a hand held up to the sunlight.

(To reconstruct a relationship of the flesh in words requires an unfamiliar architecture.)

&&&

And then, one evening, you touched me.

How your touch took me inside. How, suddenly, I felt the words of every poem I had ever read collecting on my skin like tiny beads of sweat. I was inside a single note of music, between the bristles of a paintbrush, coiled up into a reel of the most spectacular film. *When you touched me, I sank into you like blood into water.*

I would give anything to forget this moment. Such a short word, *touch,* so forgettable. As though it were spontaneous, reversible, as though it could leave no trace. In the *CH* the illusion of finality, as if to deny the way it lingers, hovers over the sentence.

& & &

How my father held me when I was a child, with some doubt, but also ease and grace, as if I were an extension of his flesh. He would carry me for hours, comfortably, and I would feel perfect and safe.

(To hold my pen in this way, to feel both reverence and agility, and a certain inevitability.)

& & &

In the desert, I thought. Where love would have to be pure, simple, dry. The hot dry wind, not like breath at all, riding the sand, fingernails along a passive back, rearranging, reconfiguring at its whim. Dunes: high, steep breasts, or low, soft hips. No grain of sand is still; the promise of rest, of leaning sleepily against another, lingers, evasive. The comforting inevitability of the wind's stark heat. And then, those days of restlessness, the sand surrendering its weight to the dry wind, the wind that needs to be not just *over* but *through*, whipping the sand up inside itself. This consummation, this obliteration.

:the way freedom is only enticing when it is windborne, a scrap of white paper on a dusty sidewalk, and you chased it, but never too fast, in case:

How love would be in this place. Arid as a second language, adjectives and adverbs superfluous in the heat. No room for insipid arguments or extraneous nouns. Prepositions irrelevant in this vast directionlessness. Words only of extremity, verbs, pronouns. Here I might have loved you better, here I might write this letter to you. All the words in all these drafts fly up in a sandstorm. I will collect a handful of sand and put it in an envelope, you will open it and pour it into your palm and there it will land, a final, perfect letter.

& & &

> I want to feel again the violent thumping inside of me, the rushing, burning blood, the slow, caressing rhythm and the sudden violent pushing, the frenzy of pauses when I hear the raindrop sounds.
>
> Anaïs Nin to Henry Miller

& & &

Is a letter that is never sent still a letter. A communication stilled, the way love is. Quelled. But I have been trying to write the letter, I have thought it, it has changed how I think about Aidan. If he never reads a final draft, does that mean it was never a letter. What if I sent it and it got lost in the mail, or he refused to read it. Does that affect its letterness. A quagmire. I think about things like this instead of thinking about Aidan. Sometimes I am so tired of thinking of him, of what I should say to him. He is beginning to grow dimmer; his words are becoming translucent. Should he fade away, what then. What then to explain this longing, this sorrow.

And so I write to keep him bright, to stave off that looming dullness. But am I really going to send Aidan a letter, or am I trying to emulate him, to be closer to him by doing what he does? And failing, because the words never mean what I want them to; they are too specific and not specific enough at the same time. I am jealous of his poetry: the clear opacity of metaphor. So I write streams of limp words, each one with less strength, less meaning than the one before, until the letters begin to wisp up into the atmosphere.

Other times I write a few empty words, like *the crescent of your hip pressing into my thigh*, and suddenly I am crying because it's so vivid and I can't stand the thought of that never happening again, although really it's just a series of words I happened to string together without thinking of him. Everything is fine and despair falls like an axe and there is nothing in the world but loss. And all the poems and letters in the world will not make this longing abate.

acenesthesia [G. *a*- priv. + *koinos,* common, + *aisthesis,* feeling]. Absence of the normal sensation of physical existence, or of the consciousness of visceral functioning.

I have changed my route home from the library so that every day I walk past the house where Aidan and I used to live. And then I walk past the café where he used to go to write and I peer in the window every day although I know his red head won't be there. Every day I leave the library at the end of my shift and I say to myself, don't walk that way, don't walk past his house, because you know he's not there any more, he doesn't live anywhere near here, and still you're disappointed. And then I walk that way, and I try to pretend I have no control over my feet but really I know I always do and I feel worse for not exercising it. I feel worse because I know I want to see him in that house because I can't imagine his new place, his new life, and I like to feel like he is still inside me, within me, even though it is so painful to have him there, and even more painful to know that he is still there because I want him to be. And then, as I walk past the café, I say to myself, don't look in to see if he's sitting there because you know he's not, and then I turn my head and I hate myself for my lack of control and I hate him for not being there and I'm relieved because if he was there he would know I was looking for him. And then I worry because I know that for so long I felt with him that he was eluding me and I thought that if only I could catch a glimpse of him without him seeing me then I would have captured him finally, and I still feel this way. I think every day that if only I didn't do this I would be *over* him, but what does that mean. How it's not about prepositions, that I have been *over* him and *under* him and *beside* him and *away from* him, and the only way I would ever be *over* him is if there were no preposition between us at all. Or just a preposition with nothing, no Aidan, on the other side of it. I am *over, under, beside, against.* Then it would be done. Meanwhile he is always there, on the other side of some preposition, even when, especially when, he is not in the house and not in the café, and I am always disappointed, and relieved.

& & &

My father would take me to the library and I would spend the afternoon choosing all the books I would read during the week. I would sit in the corner behind a large pile of books and pull my knees up to my chin, a book opened wide in front of me, a shield. And when I began to read, it would be as if there had never been anything but this story and these pictures.

(To write to you this way, disappearing in through words like a curtain until I cease to exist except through words of you. To find a language so true and satisfying it would take me to you and protect me from you at the same time.)

& & &

If I could take a photograph of that night. Grass green as words, the sky austere and uncertain and black. Stars, syllables of abandon. The insurrection of the flesh, our bodies sloped together on the hill. We talked softly, the dark keeping our words in close around us. Hot night, the damp of your palm finding my spine, pulling the wet of my back in tight to you. The incalescence of deep night, your breath tentative on my neck. An irreversibility in the way your leg fell over mine. Words, then, impertinent, futile, and I felt your body, articulate, inextricable, beside mine.

If I could take a photograph of that night, I would print it with a dark filter, so the black areas would be dark as despair and the only whites would be flashes of skin, glaring. The starkness of love. And no matter where you looked you would still see these sudden moments of irredeemable white and in them you would see what we have lost.

The photograph would be large, showing the bench where you asked me to meet you at midnight, where our empty wine bottle and the book you wanted to lend me were still sitting, and the tree we lay beneath, the shapes of leaves indiscernible in the dull moonlight. In it too would be the smell of flowers from a nearby garden and the smell of garbage from the street. The sound of a dog, muffled, from inside a house. The promise of beginning, a hint of inevitability, a palpable sense of the self quieting beneath some weight.

If I could take a photograph of that night, I would include in it all the things you ever did and said that diminished it. The shadows of every fight we ever had, disapproving looks, the darkness of failure hanging in the sky. Words of criticism extinguishing the stars, your waning interest a blur behind every blade of grass. The inextricability of love and loss, sorrow lurking, disguised, in every image.

adermia [G. *a-* priv. + *derma*, skin]. Congenital absence of skin.

Factor IX deficiency or dysfunction (hemophilia B, Christmas disease) occurs in 1 in 100,000 male births like deaths, the same column in the newspaper, and on the day my father died the word *death* left me in the way that words do— a sudden decompression, a spontaneous combustion. How they are there, but never present, unremarkable as cutlery sitting in a drawer, until the day you need a knife and you pick it up and drop it, the clatter, the explosion of light, violating your foot and suddenly it is a foreign object and you have no word to describe it, *knife* not right, no longer *accurate laboratory diagnosis is critical, since it is clinically indistinguishable from factor VIII deficiency (hemophilia A) but requires treatment with a different plasma fraction*, the way the word has splintered, *death*, still functioning in a haphazard way. Like when I was a little girl and I would stand on my father's feet and hold his hands and he would dance. A slow waltz, a tango, two pairs of feet, one motion. Like this word *death*, there was a grievous failure to adhere to the rules of the dance, we were not so graceful *either fresh frozen plasma or a plasma fraction enriched in the prothrombin complex proteins is used* to such direction I became distraught because I had thought there would always be this pattern to follow, a stencil for my actions, some counterpoint to my darkness. I had thought there might always be some buoyancy to be found among the heaviness of words like judgement and emptiness, I had not thought there was room enough in sorrow to live in *addition to the expected complications of hepatitis, chronic liver disease, and AIDS, the therapy of factor IX deficiency has a special hazard*, such a love, it asks that you imagine it will always exist. Faith, it asks; imagine, it requires, him holding my child, his grandson, his face, voice softening at the sight of him (the blood, always, the blood). Imagine how we might have argued over the car after he taught me how to drive. How such a love would test, alter, deepen, not like now, frozen always at the love of ten years old, how he would be taken, and sometimes I can find him even when I don't want to and other times, he seems to have vanished without a *trace quantities of activated coagulation factors in prothrombin complex concentrates may activate the coagulation system and cause thrombosis and embolism,* when a word, like a blood clot, catches in the throat, then I can't breathe and I feel my lungs struggle and I imagine this is how he felt that last day. How he searched, his eyes, his hands, his voice, reaching. As though he might hold himself here. My failure to contain him, to repel death. And I smelled it, I felt it, careening towards us. His face, his face and the blood, always.

& & &

Grass, bristling into my back, thousands of insurgent words. The weight of you over me like darkness, a quilt of variegated synonyms, you kiss me. I count the sweet leaves of this night, push deeper into this obfuscating dark.

Such a touch, skinless; I would abandon perfidious language for it, for you.

& & &

It was at a party where I expected to find you, my Aidan. I had told them all I hoped you wouldn't be there, that I would go in spite of you, but that was a lie. I think they knew I was going not in spite of your presence, but because of it.

I walked in the door, apprehensive. It was too bright and it had an almost forced air to it. I moved quickly through the room toward the kitchen, ending conversations before they could begin, promising to return after leaving the wine in the kitchen. I couldn't look at anyone, I was scanning the room for you. When I got to the kitchen, the host was there, and she saw my anxiety, and said don't worry, Aidan's not coming, we told him you'd be here. I feigned relief but I felt such disappointment.

They introduced me to a man named Adam. A name much like yours but for a softening, it promised gentleness, acquiescence. *M*, a prelude to *N*. I sat beside him and we began to talk. To laugh, awkwardly, at first, at being set up, a deference to these friends. He became more comfortable and it was easier. But I was so ashamed— at being alone, at being somebody my friends felt they should arrange dates for, at being unaccustomed to this. My words were stiff, awkward. I tried to ask him questions, but he could tell I was uninterested in his answers. All I could think about was how he wasn't you, about how difficult unfamiliarity is. Everything has to be explained; not like with you, where our vocabularies had converged and our references were common. I knew I was supposed to find this exhilarating, to savour the opportunity to reconfigure myself, to construct myself in some new way for this person, but I found it frightening.

We drank more quickly, and he leaned over and kissed me. The taste of beer, of cigarettes, of some tongue that was not yours. I was unsure how to respond. It felt good, in spite of the foreignness, but I quickly pulled back. I knew then it might be possible to love somebody else, and I wasn't sure if I wanted that. I didn't want this to be over, my Aidan, this sadness, this story of us, and although I knew we shouldn't be together, I felt so frightened of undertaking such a thing again. And I felt like I would be betraying you, this, if I were to kiss, to love, another, as though it would diminish or contradict how we felt.

I knew, too, that I might like this Adam, that maybe I might even love him, but I was too afraid, so I apologized and quickly left, flustered and crying. I didn't know what else to do. I went home and lay in bed and thought about how angry I was with you for making me feel this way, especially since I knew you would never feel the strange loyalty to our history that I do. And then I felt worse because I knew I was still allowing considerations of you to colour what I do and that you are not thinking of me in the same way. Such longevity, love, however false.

adiaphoria [G. *a-* priv. + *phoros,* bearing]. Failure to respond to stimulation after a series of previously applied stimuli.

And when the longing goes so deep it begins to turn itself inside out: some *is* rising, substantial, from the indurate *is not.* The *is not* a mosaic of mirrors turned inward, its quietnesses refracting over and over until the *is* emerges, loud as rain, the way words turn themselves inside out until they finally achieve meaning in their soundlessness. And when longing surrenders this ineffable core, gives forth into being its sad incandescence, then life is suddenly more terrible, an inchoate tragedy, indecorous in its persistence, and halfway in the turning-out of this word, where half the flesh is bared to the air, there is the loss of *you*, the indefatigable sorrow that is my *you.* Where the *you* rises like steam off the radiator and condenses on the raw window pane, a thin sheen between me and late autumn. What *you* has always been. Because it is at the end of autumn when this chasm of *you*, of words of *you*, runs deepest and longing turns inside out to protect itself from the insidious wind, from words stark as denuded branches, from me;

and because it is at the end of autumn when thoughts of *you* whirl towards me, away from me, arid leaves in that insidious wind, and there is no quiet in me except the quiet of the rain of leaves all around me, except the quiet of *not you.*

& & &

The morning after the party was Saturday, and I was relieved I had to go in to work at the library. Saturday is always busy, and I would have things to do all day. But I was also uneasy, because of the empty noise of the steel shelves, the way it magnifies with each breath until my head begins to throb. I lay awake so late, angry with myself for allowing you to ruin the evening. Or, rather, allowing myself to allow you to ruin it. And then I thought about Adam, imagined how his body might feel pressed against mine. How his chest might feel under my hands, how soft his morning lips might be. How if I traced the shape of his face enough I might forget yours, how my fingers remember when I'm not paying attention.

I told my co-workers I thought the fiction section needed tidying, and I spent much of the morning there, rubbing my fingers hard on the bumpy spines of stories, scraping at the memory of your skin. Each spine one vertebra, each page a cell. I tried to breathe deeply, to draw myself inside it. To be carried through its arteries, feel the lulling pulse of its centre. The soft cushion of organs, the certainty of its skeleton. Breath exhaled in perfect sentences.

I re-alphabetized the books, aligned their spines perfectly along the edge of the shelf, but it was not enough to quiet the chant of your words through my body, the throbbing sound of your name.

& & &

I would love you in the jungle. Thick and dense and green; a rampant hope. Bright flowers, incongruous as kind words, and a love deeper than the sun could shine in. A predatory dampness, decay lurking between the stalks. Contradiction like so many leaves. I touch you like fear, I smell you like rain, I hack a path out from the centre of the jungle and it would be my letter to you.

& & &

Sometimes I imagined your death.

By fire, your body lithe and graceful in the flames, writhing. The smell of you. The sound of searing flesh written through the heat. Smoke rising like lust. A thin shroud of ash over me.

By water, the waves folding you into themselves. Your body so smooth through the water, I see your flesh ripple in concentric circles. The water's desire for you, its irrepressible urge to take you, to press itself in through you. Fear rising in bubbles.

By falling, you, always so level, the air rushing past you as you careen to the ground. The inflexibility of such a path. Wind pulling at your face, its fingers through your hair. The expectation of the earth pulling you into itself.

By collision, hot metal selfish against your skin, dashing your body against itself, shaping you into its image. The lurid crack of bone, the splatter of blood against steel. The smell of tar and gasoline pushing in through your pores. The crescendo of movement, the sudden stillness.

By illness, disease easing its way through your blood. The malignant white of the hospital, of the nurses' uniforms. Each cell a betrayal, one by one, your body turning on you from the inside out. The inefficacy of sharp needles, long words, chemical assailants. Descent inevitable, heralded by the smell of decay.

By sorrow

adient [L. *adiens*, pr. p. of *adeo*, to go toward]. Having a tendency to move toward the source of a stimulus, as opposed to abient.

And then my words begin to disintegrate. Before I can say or write or even think them, they start to splinter— long, dense vowels, abrupt consonants, meandering diphthongs, the lacunae of silent letters— floating up into a cloud. Opaque, foreboding; the dark before a thunderstorm. Thin bits of light pushing through, illuminating the sounds of your name, a strong *A*, solid *D*: sounds loud as thunder, bright as lightning in this darkness.

Until the sounds crowd in so thick they begin to condense, oversaturated. One by one they bead down my face, certain and monotonous as rain.

& & &

I have been thinking about the night Aidan and I met in the park at midnight and lay under a tree, drinking wine and kissing; I have been trying to understand what made it so momentous.

How to explain the irreversible blurring of selves, how to understand the simultaneity of terror and bliss at that almost indiscernible moment of no turning back. And, at the same time, to identify within that perfection the ghosts of everything that went wrong.

I have tried to understand it in words, but they only fracture and disintegrate the everythingness; if only that night could be a photograph, and then I could scrutinize it or tear it up.

Aidan probably doesn't even remember that night, prefers not to recall the way the fact of *us* suddenly crystallized so that nothing we can ever do, no matter how far wrong everything has gone, will be able to erase it. As if it were a tray of photographic fixer, cementing us into indelibility. How to render this with the impermanence of ink, how to depict the enormity of love's failure with the fickleness of language.

& & &

How I always lost at Scrabble. We sat at the table, me with my legs crossed, you leaning back, balanced with your arm across the back of the next chair. I would plan my word during your turn; you would wait. And while you thought about your word you would turn the tiles, polished skin, over in your hand, memorizing the smoothness with your fingers. I would be impatient with you, your belief in the perfect word, and then I would look at your fingers caressing the tiles and I would feel a flash of arousal. How I wanted you to touch me that way. Gentle, appreciative, hungry.

Seven letters to tell you everything. I press my fingertips hard against them until white letters appear, raised. I hold them against your lips and spell this to you.

& & &

When I was very young, my father would sing me to sleep every night. He was tone-deaf, a terrible singer, and after he died I believed for a long time that it was through his voice that the treachery of his blood chose to manifest itself. *You are my sunshine, my only sunshine, you make me haaaaappy, when skies are grey. I'm looking over a four-leaf clover, that I've overlooked before.* I can't remember much of the songs— simple melodies, the occasional line, *Daisy, Daisy, I'm half-crazy all for the love of you,* and I'm never sure it's not something I've just made up.

(To convey the beauty of imperfection, to use the language of discordance to depict us. Love as a minor chord, a song from the forties in the wrong key. Faith in the face of this.)

& & &

Sometimes I imagine what it would be like to spend one more night with you. There are no words, nothing to take back or regret or forgive. Only silence, and through it you reach for my hand, I touch your cheek or your shoulder. And then our hands are together, or our arms are around each other, your hand caressing my side, mine clutching at your shoulder. We pull closer together, and your lips are as soft as I remember, but I am surprised by how perfectly they fit themselves to mine, the way a voice fits around a perfect word.

We might make love a thousand different ways. Tender and slow, with praises, touches, and sighs; fast and rough, with gasps and bruises. Your hands, or mine, tied. A thousand positions, a thousand gestures, a thousand permutations of love. Bittersweet, vicious, joyous: irrevocable.

Then I see it approaching, and I think *no, not this time.* Always the same ending. After we have made love, we lie together on the bed, sweaty and breathless. I curl around you, my head on your left shoulder where I feel your heart, still impatient, and I lay my hand on your stomach to feel it rise and fall, slowing. Your hand lies near mine, your palm upturned as if to catch something. I reach across you and rest the tips of my fingers upon yours. I let them lie there, to allow the whorls of my fingerprints to settle into yours. But as soon as your fingers acknowledge the weight of mine upon them, they abruptly pull away, recoiling. My fingertips fall onto your damp stomach. I curl them into my palm and pull my hand back to my side, and I move my body imperceptibly away. Your breath slows, you pretend nothing has happened, and you fall asleep. I lie beside you, thinking how I will lie awake all night to savour being beside you one last time, how I will memorize the sight of your body in the dark, how I will run my fingers over the shape of you until it is imprinted on my hands so they will always be able to summon your cheek, your elbow. I open my eyes to find that it is morning, that I have slept all night, and we lie back to back on the bright bed.

Light, disconsolate and unapologetic, privy to the dark of sorrow like some unforgiving confessor.

& & &

Wet autumn leaves, the smell of melancholy. A smell not of the inevitability of decay but of ineffable fecundity. A sorrow not of loss but of lack, of never. (Your hair.) Empty tree branches, disingenuous, searching through the wind. A false solidity, disproved by such acquiescence. (Your chest.) Daylight hushed, stilled, under the weight of such dark air; dawn more sluggish with each day. (Your hipbone, sharp, how it began to push, slice, into the vertex of my thigh.) Silence pressing in over the city; the snow, selfish, swallowing noise. White, some shroud over this. (Your hands, their soft touch on my breast, over my mouth.) Darkness, a suffocating moisture. (Your loss, the loss of

aglossia [G. *a*- priv. + *glossa*, tongue]. Congenital absence of the tongue.

When Ethan walked into the library this morning suddenly I knew what was going to happen, that he was going to ask me to go out with him. I ducked into the back room before it could happen, and I looked carefully through the stack of books to be rebound as though I were appraising them. Really I kept looking up, without raising my head, so I could watch him through the small window as he deliberately arranged his books on the desk. I tried to guess where he would ask me to accompany him. A movie, dinner; I could not imagine being with him anywhere but the library. I could not imagine how he would look outside of the warm study room. Going on a date with him, with anyone, would mean that this grief is not insurmountable and is weaker than I thought, or that I am stronger, or that I loved Aidan less than I thought. It would mean I was getting on with my life, as though life were something independent of this love and this grief. I vacillated between thinking I could never betray Aidan like that and that I wanted to. Suddenly I felt a surge of relief that this grief might be finite, and I rushed from the back room over to Ethan and smiled and waited. He looked uncertain, dismayed this might happen so easily, and told me in a casual way that he had an extra ticket to the opera on Friday, if I would like to accompany him. I paused long enough to see his consternation and then I told him I would love to go with him. His smile opened, and I felt pleased. I turned to walk away, and I was filled with an enormous regret— a regret that was fear and sadness, and bewilderment.

& & &

You would always cut yourself when you shaved. I walked into the bathroom one morning after I heard the razor clatter in the sink. You stood, helpless, watching in the mirror as your hands held your neck, blood streaming red, tracing lines down your throat. Hands red, guilt. Unrelenting blood, wet as hope; the sting of salt. You watched me in the mirror as I came towards you, bringing toilet paper to staunch the blood. I touched your shoulder, then poured water over your hands, pink swirling until the water ran clear.

& & &

You took me to the zoo because you thought I wanted to go. I didn't tell you I didn't want to go. That zoos make me sad.

We walked holding hands. It was a hot day, and our hands were sweating together, but I didn't want to pull mine away because I knew how hard you were trying to please me. Because I had told you I felt you were taking me for granted, that I didn't feel like you appreciated me. As though taking me out and holding my hand for a day were enough to make me feel loved. Not understanding that I would be more moved if you remembered how much sugar I like in my tea or if you looked at me the way you used to or if you meant it when you asked how my day was. Instead we walked past the cages in the zoo with sweaty hands. You were so enthusiastic, pointing at the animals, the antics of the monkeys, the ferocity of the lions, the languor of the polar bears. You paused in front of the mating mourning doves but I hurried you along, uncomfortable. I could tell you had a growing sense of dismay, but I could not quell the torpor of my body. My heartbeat was low and deep and my lungs felt shrunken, reluctant inside my ribcage. Every movement was a struggle against the swell of desolation. I watched the tiger pacing; I imagined I could feel his eyes lock with mine. You asked what was wrong and I couldn't explain it. I lied and said it was the heat. Your disappointment was palpable; I summoned some energy, smiled, and we continued.

& & &

Perhaps I can sing you this letter, notes clear and long in place of my discordant words. The sincerity of perfect harmony; the impermanence of song.

To begin I inhale deeply, my chest rising as if towards you; I breathe in until I feel the air go ragged as torn paper. The music is in front of me, a pattern of black notes, the results from some polygraph, your body the staff the notes explore like fingers, and I close my eyes. I open my mouth and begin to sing to you, and in the instant between the hard push of breath and the sound of the first note there are all the ways I tried to love you and all the ways I tried to forget you, and then there would be music. True and loud and clear, baritone, tenor, alto, soprano all at once, some perfect note that is everything I have ever wanted to tell you. A note so honest I feel the air shift to make room for it, a note that sets every cell of your body ringing. No words; language gutted of its consonants, leaving only the pure viscera of vowels. These I sing to you in random order, spelling out all the ways that we touched one another.

And when I finish singing this to you, my Aidan, it would be over. There would be no trace of it. My love, my grief, my regret would have dissipated with the last echoes of my song. There would be nothing to reread on a sad rainy afternoon, no record of its success or failure, nothing to touch. There would be only the memory in my lungs of the breath that held you, and some quiet melody that might haunt me in my deepest sleep.

agnosia [G. ignorance; from *a-* priv. + *gnosis,* knowledge]. Agnea; lack of sensory-perceptual ability to recognize objects.

The chaos of this becomes even more apparent to me when I am surrounded by the orderliness of the library. Books lined up along the edges of the shelves, taunting me like some perfect paragraph. Sometimes I hide in a corner where everyone thinks I am shelving or sorting or tidying, and I pick books at random from the shelf. Usually I choose them for their titles, especially titles that are long and almost sentences. First I admire the cover and the title, and then before I open each one I imagine what the writing will be like, and I wonder if it will be like yours. I imagine how you would start a book with such a title, the perfect order of your words. The arc of a single sentence breathtaking enough to replay itself over and over in my mind for a whole day. And I imagine how I would feel if I had written it, how safe I would feel if I knew I could write a sentence like that. To know I had such a sentence in me would make me mean something, would make me larger than all my petty obsessions with you, would make me forget you, even if the sentence were about you. Then I think I'm going to start to cry because I know I don't have such a sentence inside me, and here I am shelving the books of those who do, and all I can think is how if I had the power to write such transcendent words they would carry me safely away from you. How even if I had such articulable beauty inside me, it would be, always, about you.

& & &

I imagined it was forty years from now and my telephone rang and it was you. After so many years. I was not surprised to hear from you although we hadn't spoken in so long.

What I hated was the warmth in my voice. That there was forgiveness and familiarity and love in the sound of my voice. That we spoke to each other as if only a single breath had passed in all that time. You treated me so softly, with such nostalgia and regret in your words, and for an instant I believed you had been present throughout my entire life. How simple it had been then, you said, when we were so young, and I nodded through the phone and I hated myself for it, for wanting to believe you, and for hearing your tears, and for again being complicit in your narrative. When I hung up the phone and went back to whoever it is that I loved then, I felt tears down my cheeks and I hated you for always being there. Always the third point of some obtuse triangle; however I love another, you loom, a vacant presence, hinging and separating.

& & &

When I was packing my boxes, I found, in a pile of photographs, the small St. Christopher medallion you had left behind. I reached for the phone to call and tell you I had it, that I would return it to you, but I changed my mind and put the phone back down. It made me think of the small boy I imagined you to have been— enthusiastic, beautiful, lonely, odd. And how there are still vestiges of these things in you, showing themselves in rare moments of honesty. These are the things I loved about you most.

St. Christopher with his staff, protecting children, carrying them to safety. Small, tin; I pressed the medallion into my palm until I couldn't feel it any more; the way I love you. I decided to keep it, and I put it in my drawer. Now I take it out sometimes when I think of you; when I hate you it makes me relent and cry, and when I am sad it makes me hate you for losing it, and yourself.

& & &

When my father died, my mother lost her words. After the funeral, after all the cruel details, after everyone thought we'd be all right. Suddenly my mother fell silent, paralyzed, and lay in bed for two weeks. Immobile, unable to utter a word, unable to hear a sound. Me, at ten, sitting beside her on the bed, crying; I was so frightened, and envious. A shield of silence. I wondered if she was hearing something else instead, the wail of ambulances, the nurses' chatter, my brother's questions, my father's last quiet words to her. Every argument they'd ever had, every kind word, the sound of his fist against the wall, his moans. Or maybe she could hear all of these things, a cacophony of sounds inside every letter.

(To write this way, a keening lament and a sharp curse in every syllable.)

& & &

On a mountain. Where love would have to be rarefied, precarious. Rocks, uncertain as promises, solid as disbelief. A stream, cold, honest, winding down towards sea level; the way the mountain shoulders this inevitability, the insistence of gravity. How my body sinks into you like trust. Air thin as conviction.

Dawn, earlier on one side of the mountain, the light, the shadows always uneven. Lichen, invasive like doubt.

:the way your body caved into mine, how you denied this avalanche, refuted the inconstancy of the escarpment. How you thought solidity was a virtue:

How love might be in this place. Solitary as a tree, slow and certain and plush as moss. Unobtrusive as light. Paths clear as grammar, routes laid out like some familiar language. Verbs sure-footed, nouns irrelevant pebbles. Adjectives and adverbs thinned out with the oxygen, there is breath only for the certitude of action. Description, superfluous. How we would breathe, speak, so slowly and deeply in this place. A piece of rock, unencumbered by ambiguity; I will seal it into an envelope.

agraphia [G. *a*- priv. + *grapho,* to write].
Anorthography; logagraphia; impairment of the ability to write.

A semantic strangulation, a cloying adherence to the constraints of grammar, the paralysis imposed by structure. Strictures of grammar incompatible with the chaos of our love. Words smothered into the rigid shapes of sentences, as relentlessly formulaic as our lovemaking had become. An unvaried rhythm, too familiar. *subject verb object,* caress penetrate eject. To fall out of language the same way you fall out of love.

Grammarless.
A grammarless letter. Forego the etiquette of indentation,
the proprieties of the paragraph.
resist punctuation
clauses   strings of words   strewn over the page your red
hair splayed

across my pillow

stray memories a photograph a
smile

synaesthesia a conflation of all you are it was I am

how to depict loss by adding

a collage of clauses written in pencil
you erase them one by
not linear not circular
words on a page patternless
asymmetrical

a distillation of absence

how to depict the softness of your
skin in the angularity of letters, to depict the harshness of
your voice in a
comma's gentle curve?

becoming stifled
Aidan
violation

acquiescence again

a ceramic ardour a vicious monotony

a dog

a father

laughing into the morning

But how would you assemble these?

The myth of coherence, of discreteness, it assumes a mechanical simplicity. A full box of magnetic letters, an alphabet of intentions and failures. Purgation, accumulation. Accretion. Reliance on the deception of order, the faithlessness of chaos. The hypocrisy of language; the contradiction of such a letter. Choking on the rules; adrift without them.

& & &

My beloved Aidan,

Last night: did you know?

I saw him at a poetry reading. His poems were terse, violent. Release denied, accumulation. Sensual and succinct. So different than yours, my Aidan, and I loved him for it. After he read, I approached him and told him how much I enjoyed hearing him. He told me he was happy to see me and proud of me, and hugged me tight to him and I felt his breath in my hair. I felt overwhelmed, the sudden presence of something that has been savoured as an absence. I have been attracted to him for some time, Aidan, imagined lying naked with him, loving him both for himself and for what he means to you. *I'm so glad you came to my reading*, he said. He looked into my eyes when he said this. *I've been thinking about you a lot*, he said. *About how I'd like to spend more time with you, to know you not through Aidan but as yourself.* This startled and pleased me. I leaned in closer to him and breathed in slowly, as though I might become accustomed to him this way, taking him in, his smell, a little at a time. I sat with him and we drank some wine until it was late. Without talking about it, we arrived at his apartment. He put some music on, something loud and thumping, and he walked toward me.

I've been waiting for this, I thought. Anticipating, speculating. How he might touch me— rough, quick, like his poetry, or soft, lyrical, like some hidden self. How he would sleep— defiant, on his back, or curled up, fearful. Whether he would brush his teeth before he kissed me, whether he kept his condoms beside the bed. He kissed me and quickly undressed himself and then me, and then made love to me, neither roughly nor tenderly, not fast or slowly. I was disappointed. His movements were all deliberate, rehearsed. I did not feel his poems in the way he touched me, nor did I find some secret self, some part of him hidden deeper than his writing that only I would see, that I could hold always as mine.

I could feel you there, my Aidan. I could sense your presence in his motions. I was afraid he thought I was with him only because it would take me closer to you or because I was seeking vengeance on you. Both of these are true, in part, but I was fond of him and attracted to him as well. I knew he felt guilty, as though he had betrayed you, and he suggested you needn't know about it.

I left his apartment in the morning. He had no time to have breakfast with me. I walked home, wearing my crumpled clothes of the night before, still smelling of stale smoke and of him, my hair oily and tangled. I felt happy. I was walking down the bright streets, thinking about loving him. Before I reached my street, however, I felt my mood sink. By the time I stepped into my apartment, I could feel tears running down my cheeks. I came into my cold apartment and before I even took off my coat I sat down and sobbed. I cried for a long time without knowing why. And I realized that maybe I had done this because I wanted to feel closer to you, but that, in fact, it took you further away from me. And more than that, I was crying because I had expected something grander, something that might fill the empty space in me. I realized then that nothing could ever fill that space. And I cried because I knew I had asked too much of you and I had ruined everything. That it might always be this way.

& & &

> You are testing my courage to the full, like a torturer. How to extricate myself from this nightmare? I have only one source of strength (*humanly*, I have no strength), I have only writing, and it is this which I am doing now with a desperation you can never conceive of— I am writing *against* myself, *against* what you may call my imperfections, *against* the woman, *against* my humaneness, *against* the continents which are giving way.
>
> Anaïs Nin to Henry Miller

& & &

The way that the flame is tethered to the wick.

Seaweed drying into prophecies on the sand. Edges curling as we walk by, telling of your ebb— as the shoreline recedes, so too will you. Despair is always premonitory. Against this, the sand is more articulate than I, it clings to your feet with an insistence mimicked only by your insidious faith in words. As though the sound of your soft reassurances could warm your silent touch. As though the extravagance of three monosyllables were enough. I look up, away from your voice. The waning moon is visible even now, at midday, and the sky darkens at the sound of you; the water refuses the remaining sunlight, hurling it back at the sky in blinding darts. These things are wiser than words, I am too old not to believe in signs.

The way that the breath is drawn into the lungs.

It might be reluctantly, in the solicitude of night, the way you leave me, or effortlessly, some windy day. In the opacity of late afternoon cloud. Soon or twenty years from now. With a gentle touch, a quick stab, a false word, nothing. I imagine a thousand lives for you, a thousand lovers. I look over at you, there is a pallor of silence to your frantic words. Your vocabulary settling into stillness like an unwilling corpse. Streaks of poverty in your voice, and I tremble before the eloquence of these omens. Their voices always keening, the soft sound of loss infecting me. Warning, always, that you will leave me, that no word is unopposed, that every tale can be a lament.

The way that the sand is pulled into the tide.

I imagine your bloated corpse tangled into a blanket of seaweed, fetid water filling every crevice where your love for me used to be. Filigree of green around your neck. A thin coating of white salt over your skin, drawing all the moistness of my love from you. The soft smell of decay your cologne. Your reassurances settling into the still bowl of your heart to rot. There is comfort in this quiet, it will warm me in your absence.

The way that the words are bound to the page.

AIDS. Acquired immunodeficiency syndrome; a disease characterized by opportunistic infections (e.g., *Pneumocystis carinii* pneumonia, candidiasis, isosporiasis, cryptococcosis, toxoplasmosis) and malignancies (e.g., Kaposi's sarcoma, non-Hodgkin's lymphoma) in immunocompromised persons; caused by the human immunodeficiency virus transmitted by exchange of body fluids (e.g., semen, blood, saliva) or transfused blood products; hallmark of the immunodeficiency is depletion of T4+ helper/inducer lymphocytes, primarily the result of selective tropism of the virus for these lymphocytes.

What if he wants to touch me, I think. What will I do if he tries to touch me. I am paralyzed by this thought, I can't imagine what I will do if he touches me, even by accident. All day at work I have been thinking this and I am starting to feel my heart beat through my head and my stomach thicken with worry. Through this, I make myself dress and walk to the restaurant where I have agreed to meet Ethan for dinner before the opera. I sit down and we order food, although I am sure I will be unable to eat. We begin to talk, and I find myself enjoying it. He is smart and witty, he tells amusing anecdotes and offers sharp insight. And he listens intently to me— like you often did not do, Aidan. Every word of our conversation is enjoyable, and yet I am still preoccupied with my fear. I choreograph every movement so that he is the farthest possible distance from me at any moment. At the same time, I am eager not to offend him or have him notice how strangely I am behaving. After dinner, we take a cab to the opera and find our seats, all without even the slightest inadvertent contact. We sit in the lighted hall and talk and look at our programmes until the lights are dimmed and the orchestra begins tuning. Now my fear is at its most acute. Sitting in the dark cacophony, I am tormented by how irrational this fear is. It was only a short time ago that I slept with Aidan's friend. I had let him touch and explore and fuck me. I had not hesitated to allow him access to my body; I had not even considered the possibility of refusal. For some reason I cannot understand, this is different. In my unease, I tuck my elbow under the armrest where it is inaccessible. I almost miss the beginning of the opera. *La Bohème.* I enjoy the music, I admire the loftiness of the characters' pursuit of art: not catharsis but creation. The pettiness of this letter. Against your sublime poetry, Aidan. I look beside me and Ethan is still there, entranced by Mimi's aria, and I am still terrified he will touch me and suddenly I think I am afraid because his touch will prove to me that I am here. It will remind me that it's not your touch, my Aidan, that it will never be again. The words of your poems through your fingertips. There is some small part of me that wants this, that urges my elbow out onto the armrest where Ethan might encounter it and it might begin. I swallow hard and it subsides. I close my eyes and I hear you singing to me, my Aidan, and I pull my arms close and safe against my body and I feel myself start to go numb and I succumb to the music.

& & &

Swan Lake, the most precise of the classical ballets, the most demanding. The corps de ballet strung across the stage like paper snowflakes; breaking pattern again and again, flirting with chaos, but symmetry always prevails— the breath held until a shape re-emerges. The betrayal of Siegfried is insignificant beside this white display of solidarity, their movements so fluid against the stiff tulle of the tutu. Hands so cygnet-like and graceful I begin to believe that swans have arms. The dream of every little girl, to dance both Odette and Odile in a single body, to wear the whirling black and the tragic white in a single evening.

Remember, Aidan, when I took you to the ballet, to *Swan Lake*. I thought you could love this perfection, its absolute inflexibility, the way I do. I wanted to share with you the simplicity of the ballet class, where beauty is everything. The purity of form. Nothing is relevant but the striving for aesthetic perfection. One hand resting gently on the barre, the other softly curved, lowered, *bras bas*, feet in first position, heels together, toes pushing apart towards a straight line. The piano, and begin. *Arms in second demi-plié and up grand plié and up relevé and down*

Remember how you thought it was dull, the plot facile, the characterizations flaccid. Discomfort at the absence of words; you were blind to the language of gesture. You didn't see the joy of the possibility of perfection within each motion.

The precision of choreography. No movement left unplanned, every beat accounted for. No room at all in the expanse of the stage for a human voice, no place for words in such a full language.

& & &

How touch wasn't enough, how we tangled ourselves together to maximize surface-area contact. How we still wanted more.

In the beginning, we always made love like that. Our mouths never separating except to explore, briefly, neck elbow stomach breast thigh, and then mouth again, like home. Bodies together like pages in a book; ecstasy as much in the idea of touch as in the physical touch itself. The aphrodesia of hope, the promise of connectedness. The illusion of irrevocability. We made love like it could never be undone. Mouths together, and I would open my eyes to watch you come, the shudder of breath, eyes wild.

After it was over I would feel you still inside me, the contractions of my muscles slowing with your pulse. And, once, when you reached down to hold the condom as you pulled out, your body stiffened, and I gasped as I realized I could feel your warm semen inside me. The crushing fear of disease, of pregnancy; the pleasure of this greatest intimacy, more than touch.

& & &

When I was young, my father would take me to the marina so we could look at the boats. First we would stand on the shore and look at them, thoroughly and with reverence, and then we would walk up and down the docks. He would give me all the particulars of each boat as he ran his hand along the hull, the railings. I knew by the way he had to touch each one that he wanted a boat more than anything else in the world.

(To write to you with a caress of my hand along the ribs to articulate my longing, with a vocabulary of piers and hulls, buoyancy and rudders.)

& & &

Often I wish there were some other in this, some aperture through this by which I might understand. Someone you or I might have loved, a pinpoint of light I might direct my eye to in this dark longing. That we might have been obedient to some conventional narrative.

(A dark road, silence. You are walking towards me and you gently drop her hand. She is beautiful, not beautiful enough, and each cell in my body convulses because I see the slow rustle of her long hair in your every movement and I hear the saltiness of her skin in your every word.)

(I have told you I am meeting an old friend and you walk past the window of the restaurant where I hold hands with my lover. I feel latitude and longitude reverse within you and I am desperate and relieved to conform to this pattern, to balance this arabesque my life has become, arm and leg at odds around some uncertain centre.)

As though blame were more than the accidental confluence of five inexorable letters, as though *guilt* were more than an inchoate trellis for an inadequate sorrow.

alalia [G. *a-* priv. + *lalia*, talking]. Loss of the power of speech through impairment in the articulatory apparatus.

A moon the colour of old, stars like aberrant punctuation. Water, dark and heavy as judgement, spells this sentence back into the sky. I try to connect stars into shapes, to read meaning into this black ambiguity. To remember what the sky looked like before you, to see again the outline of you there, some stellar portent of the you that is not even you any more. The same emptiness now; that time with you an astronomical anomaly.

That night, early autumn, early love. We sat on a bench beside the lake. Water rippling like time, deep as certainty. A tedious belief in a vocabulary of love. Hopes, desires, expectations; as though these were more than the tauntings of a cruel language. As though love were some algebraic equation, some combination of linguistic variables we might balance. As though we were the first, infallible.

& & &

The overwhelming fact of this letter, how it tears at me. The disorder of it. Even in my sleep, now. I have been dreaming of you, my Aidan; sometimes we are kind and forgiving to one another, and sometimes I imagine that you are bludgeoning me with an axe. Or I, you. And often, just before I wake up, I dream the perfect letter to you, sentence by sentence. Each word fits itself in, as though it were finding its way home, its meaning bending until it shapes itself to my intention. Then, just when the letter is exactly the shape of everything I want to say, I wake up suddenly and I can never remember a word of it. Except *Aidan*, but only with the old meaning. On the mornings when I awake with the elusive memory of such a dream, it is more difficult to force myself to go to work. I push myself up through the haze of possibility, the incontrovertible truth of the existence of such a finely honed language, a perfect letter; I push myself up through it into the day, into the library. Books, there, ordered, taunting. Each in its unique place determined by subject, author, call number, the strict linearity of the alphabet. And within each book, chapters, carefully arranged in a numerical sequence. Each and every sentence a meticulous positioning of individual words. Nothing left to chance, every word assigned a place, a function. Row upon row, page upon page, shelf upon shelf of dutiful, obedient words, each the bearer of some certain meaning. Some days I am tormented by the definitiveness of it all, thinking of the way words shuffle themselves, redefining, devolving, in my dreams and in this letter.

Perhaps I will take one word from each book here that reminds me of you, I will cut them out with scissors and drop them into a white envelope. You will open it and they will fall onto your desk, landing assuredly into the perfect sentence.

& & &

In a valley, where love would have to be sheltered, insignificant. The wind high above, teasing, an eavesdropped conversation. Grass, green and thick and undisturbed, anxious at the morning's delay, how the sun stutters its way over the crest each dawn. How your hand, tentative and warm, first touched my elbow. A verdant respite in a sequence of peaks, a secret, a reprieve. How anger, unquenched, might settle low between the blades of grass; how the stillness might swallow words before they are heard.

:the way the land lies nestled among the hills; how I slept pressed against you, sheltered by the soft slope of your side, protected, forgettable, the shadow of your indifference stretching longer and longer across me:

How love would be in this place. Lush and deep as green, lonely as a bird's cry. Slow as a paragraph, with words that are breathy and deliberate. Adjectives small and bright and wild as flowers, verbs strong and sparse as trees. Grammar resolute as your perfidiousness. All the words we should never have said thickening in the air each night until they are too heavy for the dawn and they bead on each blade of grass. I would pick some small wildflowers and sprinkle them with these drops of dew and put them in an envelope; you would spread the bright pulp of petals onto your hand and it would spell my letter to you.

& & &

The musculature of despair.

Skin thick with fear, a skeletal melancholy, confounded by flesh.

To bore in through tight pores with words sharpened like needles; this new name, *Ethan.* It scrapes at the skin, an abrasion of syllables, deeper and deeper with each phoneme until this name, this *Ethan,* has penetrated me, until the sounds have realigned themselves, whole, inside me.

Irrefutable, anatomical.

Words, thin and uncertain as breath.

alethia [G. *a*- priv. + *lethe*, forgetfulness]. Rarely used term for an incapacity to forget past events.

A vision of you, standing in our kitchen, washing dishes. A splash of red hair against your sweaty forehead, sweater sleeves pushed up to your elbows. Your voice, loud, resplendent, singing to the radio. A moment that is solitary, final, as I walk through the doorway.

Time opens like hipbones.

& & &

I knew Ethan would call to ask me for another date. I knew, too, that he had sensed my reticence and would wait a few days before calling so as not to seem overly enthusiastic. I had enjoyed our evening at the opera and I knew I should have called to thank him. I had his number on a scrap of paper by the phone, but I couldn't bring myself to call or even to copy the number into my address book.

When he called I was reading a book of poetry that frustrated me because it wasn't very good. When I answered the phone, I heard a strange voice and knew it was Ethan before he asked for me. He didn't sound like you. For a second I thought about how I loved your voice and how I couldn't love anyone who didn't have your voice. But then I was afraid, too, that I would hear your voice in his, you whispering at me in the dark, yelling from the shower, arguing with someone, often me, over the phone.

We talked for a long time, and I found myself trying hard to make him like me, although I knew he already did, and part of me didn't want him to. I was trying, like some high-school girl, to be smart and funny, and pinching my leg every time I said something stupid. As we talked, I flipped absentmindedly through the book of bad poems, and near the end I found a photograph you must have used as a bookmark. And then I was juxtaposing the sound of Ethan's voice with this picture of you and me. I imagined Ethan's arm casually over my shoulders like that, thinking how different it would feel because he is shorter than you and skinnier. How Ethan wouldn't know exactly where I liked you to put your hand. And I imagined having a conversation with you as I talked to him, thinking that you would never talk about this particular subject, or how you often interrupted me. Thinking that Ethan could never say anything as funny as that thing you said, or that you never listened so intently to me as he is doing. And I remembered how exasperated I would feel because you always had to be right and you always made me feel like I was suffocating under all the things I was trying to say but could never say well enough.

While I was still looking at the picture, Ethan asked me if I would like to go to the art gallery with him. There was a photography exhibit there I had mentioned wanting to see. I wanted not to go, I wanted to stay quietly in my apartment and write you this letter because without it this can never be over. I agreed nevertheless to meet him two days later in front of the gallery. I looked at our photograph again, and put it at the bottom of a drawer before it made me cry.

(The relentlessness of decay and of despair: sorrow's half-life.)

& & &

Your voice, loud as disappointment; and your movements. Clumsy as love. You were always breaking things. My glasses, once, left on the bed for your heavy hands to find. A door. A couple of plates, spaghetti tumbling to the floor, evisceration. A chair. All my grandmother's wine glasses; one slammed to the table too dramatically, two kicked over, two dropped, one shattered while you were washing it, your too-large fist too tightly inside until the glass burst outward shredding your hand, dishwater turning pink. Faith.

& & &

When I was three, my father took me to the circus. A tawdry small-town circus, in the hockey arena. First taste of cotton candy, pink and sweet and airy. The smell of dung, of elephant hide, old sweat. I was in love with the animals, their differentness, their thick odour, their acquiescence. There were clowns, funny, menacing. Big shoes, garish costumes, faces hidden behind make-up, unreal smiles. Disingenuous. One clown singled me out, ran up the stairs to us and honked a horn. I was frightened, and my father smiled encouragingly at me. I cried, aware suddenly that my father might not always be on my side.

(To seek vengeance on you this way. Betrayal lurking behind some cosmetic language. To make you believe that my love for you was always as cumbersome as those shoes, to make you know you are alone.)

& & &

I will paint you this letter, articulate brushstrokes in place of my colourless words.

Canvas, more pliant and forgiving than paper, rough as the skin over your knuckles, and I stretch it over the skeletal frame. I set it upon the easel and I imagine the shapes of all the letters I could write to you, coloured syllables flashing against the white. Next I prepare my palette, wood smooth as the inside of your forearm, and I squeeze paint onto it, perfect circles of cadmium red, cerulean blue, viridian, like words that have never been spoken. With my brush I defile them, blend them into a perfect sentence and I begin to paint. As I hold the brush I imagine your body in front of me and the canvas takes on the contours of you. I hold in my mind a picture of all the words I want to say to you, in their perfect order, and I paint that shape. The smell, dense and heady, makes me desire you, and I paint that in; anger, too, and sadness, as if I could brush these indelibly upon your body itself. I give a shape to all those things that have no shape, and it is the shape of you. A flesh of paint upon a skeleton of grief, the colours of love and skin and loss.

I would varnish the finished painting and then it would be done, sealed. I would hang it on my wall, where every day it would remind me of the finished story of you, my Aidan, and I would run my fingers over it to hear the perfect words of you.

alexia [G. *a*- priv. + *lexis*, a word or phrase]. Word or text blindness; visual aphasia (1); loss of the ability to grasp the meaning of written or printed words and sentences. Also called **optical, sensory**, or **visual a.**, in distinction to **motor a.** (anarthria), in which there is loss of the power to read aloud although the significance of what is written or printed is understood.

If I were ever to finish this letter. What if. Like the inevitable, dubious finality of a touch. I imagine myself folding the paper, pressing my words in on themselves. And I place it in an envelope, already labelled with your address in the centre, mine in the corner. As if this were about *to* and *from*. Two small words, all the space in the universe, and I think about us lying in bed, your soft, sticky cock pressed against me; there was no room here for *to* and *from*. And I would seal the envelope, tongue soft against the woody paper, and I would hold it tightly, as if there were some last thing to be wrung from it. I imagine standing in front of the mailbox, red like your hair, like blood, uncertain if I can send the letter, just drop it in this metal box like some bill payment. Anti-climax. I feel it slide through my fingers, rattling carelessly against the steel sides of the box. And then, quiet. And then.

& & &

> Methinks I could write a volume to you; but all the
> language on earth would fail in saying how much, and
> with what disinterested passion, I am ever yours.
>
> Richard Steele to Mary Scurlock

& & &

If I were to finish this letter, if it were ever to be done. And if I were to send it. What would you do when you opened your mailbox and this letter was there. Finished.

Would you tear it up before reading it, would you stuff it in a book to read later. Would you tell some new love, to show her how insignificant I am to you. Would you cry, wistful, would you write back in anger.

The soft spread of obsession. The way a womb, pregnant, is distended into inevitability, the only return, apocalyptic.

& & &

Comfort in the restlessness of the water, the way it folds and refolds itself around my body, the trepidation of your last touch. The way the water cannot take the moonlight straight, reflecting and refracting and shattering it into tiny fragments. To submerge myself in the blackness around these shards of moon, to go so deep into the darkness of the lake that my movements are silenced by the water before the ripples reach the surface. The water folding and refolding itself so silently I become a part of it, aware of my alienness only when the water breathes and shimmers around a passing fish. The cool sadness of the night air on my skin when I break the surface; I stay under longer and longer until my lungs burn, and in that moment of indecision when I cannot come up and I cannot stay down then my body floats up of its own will. An aria of muffled sounds under the water, and when I surface they distinguish themselves into your words, floating up like air bubbles, breaking into the cold air.

& & &

With his death, my father left my mother where words could not find her.

(If only I could write that wordlessness. Orphaned by

language, a mesh of gestures to catch the air. Sleeplessness, tears, strength, a fist clutching at nothing in the night: my letter.)

& & &

How can I see Ethan again. How can I. How can I stand beside him and not think that he is you. Not instinctively touch him like I would you. How can I bear to be beside him when he doesn't look or sound or smell or feel like you. How can I stand it if he does.

How to learn to read Ethan while I have not yet found the final chapter of you. To unravel the intricacies of two narratives; to find a home between new covers. How to overcome this new dyslexia, reading backwards, upside down, inside out, until some new language emerges. The words flashing in and out of focus, blurring, disappearing, rearranging themselves; how then to decipher them.

How can I sit beside him, breathe the air he has exhaled, feel his warmth and his smell when he is not you, and the air and the warmth and the smell of you still infect my blood, sad and skulking through my veins.

(Absence, impenetrable and hollow as bone; a skeletal grief.)

amimia [G. *a-* priv. + *mimos,* a mimic]. Loss of the power to express ideas by gestures or signs.

Words have been evaporating. So often, lately, I have begun to say a word, drawn a breath, opened my mouth, shaped my lips into that word only to find it has dissolved. Like salt in water, the phonemes still stinging the tongue, the water more viscous but no trace of the word is left but its taste. I have begun to think I need to capture my words, pin them down, staple them into my vocabulary. To subjugate them. To do this, I have started to count them, to catalogue all the words I know that I might never lose them. No dictionary. I begin where everything does.

a, ask, absent, as, Aidan, against, across, and, at, apart, admiring, around, ache, atrophied, acquiesce, am, almost, assemble, away, accumulate, accommodate, account, always

& & &

I would love you in a field. I would pick every stalk of wheat and split the husk of every grain and inside I would find every word of every letter I might write to you. I would grind them together and use the flour to bake a loaf of bread: this will be my letter to you.

& & &

> There is torture in words, torture in their linking &
> spelling, in the snail of their course on stolen paper, in their
> sound that the four winds double, and in my knowledge of
> their inadequacy. With a priggish weight on the end, the
> sentence falls. All sentences fall when the weight of the
> mind is distributed unevenly along the holy consonants &
> vowels... I wonder whether I love your word, the word of
> your hair... the word of your voice. The word of your
> flesh, & the word of your presence...
>
> Dylan Thomas to Pamela Hansford Johnson

& & &

One day you told me how much pleasure it gave you to watch me sleep, how you would wake in the night and lie quietly beside me with your eyes open. The satisfaction of my regular breaths, the silence. My utter vulnerability. And while I understood that, even enjoyed doing the same with you, I stopped being able to go to sleep with you. I used to savour the way we would, especially after making love, curl up and fall asleep at almost the same moment. That bliss of safety, release. And after you told me that, I would lie awake, feigning sleep, reciting lists, poems, numbers in my head to keep from drifting off, until I felt you give in to sleep. I would wait a bit and turn my back to you, curled in a ball where you could see less of me, before I would sleep. It was overreacting, to be sure, but I couldn't shake that feeling of violation. That you would be witness to my surrender. That you could see part of me I would never be able to see. Perhaps I make strange motions, talk in my sleep, snore. The rapid movements of my eyes. A fear not that you would hurt me (press hard on my eyes, my throat) but that you would know these things.

& & &

Perhaps I can dance you this letter, the clarity of motion in place of my hapless words.

A small movement of the hand, a cursive arch of fingers. Uncertainty opaque as ink. The foot slowly points, an inarticulable memory. My arms reach out, one in front one behind, the right leg pulls taut and begins to lift. The torso bends into this movement, this... the name of the step forgotten. Thoughts clumsy and laboured, the weight of self-consciousness.

Then I am bending further and further, reaching towards the name of this, toward words of you *penché* this is a penché and I wobble. The words now, coming to me before the shapes they signify. *glissade fouetté assemblé brisé.* Faster and my knees begin to ache my arms can no longer hold themselves up my feet stepping on one another. Stiff as prose.

A ballet lesson for you, my love.

plié the body rigid erect pried slowly open the knees spread themselves apart

développé toes pull up into a retiré and the leg slowly unfolds out to the front or side or back reluctantly as though it were being torn away

arabesque one leg lifted out high to the back straining the same side arm following the leg to the back the opposite arm pulling to the front the body forked in indecision

échappé legs together a sharp jump landing feet apart an escape

These steps will be my letter to you— a vocabulary outside of narrative, a reconsideration of semantics. A revision of grammar. Most articulate in the phonemes, longing spelled out in the angle of the wrist. A tilt of the head a more compelling adjective than *sorrowful.*

Because ballet is about suspension, I show you my heart weightless and heavy since we parted. The ballerina holds her body, holds her every move as though she were between the up and down on a swing pushed too high, in that moment when the chains slacken, the swing the heart the breath all pause as if to forge such weightlessness into tangibility. Ballet asks you to believe in that moment, in sustained flight. To forget how the body finds comfort in symmetry, how every movement of a limb away from the centre is a risk, a betrayal of equilibrium.

But my dance would be a dance not of buoyancy but of indolence, not a celebration of reach but a frightened resistance to flight. The body confounded by asymmetry. No less turgid than all these drafts. Such a weight to my body it could never leave the floor, efforts at leaping, at abandon, quelled by the density of the flesh. Feet heavy as words.

anaphia [G. *an-* priv. + *haphe*, touch]. Anhaphia; absence of the sense of touch.

A wide aperture, a slow shutter, a sharp flash: openings for doubt.

Do you remember that photograph of us together in the garden? Your arm heavy across my shoulders, uncertainty furtive and impatient under every leaf.

I met Ethan at the art gallery after work. I waited for him on the steps outside. The sun shone brightly and warmed the stone, and the sky was clear and blue, as if to assuage my anxiety. I had been uneasy all day at the library, trying to decide if I should cancel the date or not. Every time I picked up a book, I would open it to any page and choose a word at random, hoping I would find there an answer or a sign. But I always got words like "plumber" or "epistemological" or "shrubbery" that I could make no sense of. I wanted to see the photographs at the gallery, and Ethan, but I was afraid I would be encouraging him, and myself. I decided to see him again in spite of that. I was concerned, too, about what I had worn— a long skirt with a sweater that was dressy and a bit tight. I was worried such an outfit might be too encouraging, that what I was wearing might have suggested I was interested in pursuing a relationship or at least having sex because I had made some effort to look attractive, although both those reasons may have been true. In any case, I didn't have time to return home to change.

I was hoping he wouldn't show up, or that he would be late, so I would have some reason to dislike him, to reject him. Of course he was punctual, and he looked extremely attractive, with black jeans, a leather jacket, and his short blond hair. He brought me a book of poetry he had recommended, and when I opened the cover I found a pressed white rose. It was beautiful, frozen at the moment of its perfection, petals white and crisp. Such an overt indication of his intentions both pleased and troubled me, but in spite of my fear I softened my voice and thanked him for the gift.

As we entered the gallery, he opened the door for me, and touched the middle of my back as I passed him. It was the first time he had touched me. It was a gesture of familiarity and respect, and I was startled because you never touched me like that. I felt my breath catch, and I missed all the ways you ever touched me and all the ways you never would, and then I thought about learning someone else's vocabulary of touches, and I was afraid and eager at the same time. So I tried to make myself think of walking through that door as a symbolic movement, a new beginning, and that Ethan's touch should erase all the touches before, but I couldn't believe it because this letter lurks, incomplete, in my every word and movement, and so do you.

The photography exhibit was breathtaking, although I thought Ethan might have been a bit uncomfortable because the photographs were so disturbing. The subjects were bound and nude, surrounded by sinister-looking medical equipment. Intricate patterns of foliage framed the bodies, and created a malevolent pastoral. The photographs were spectacular and unnerving; they were menacing but erotic at the same time, and it was uncomfortable to realize they were arousing as well. I felt particularly uneasy because of the attraction Ethan and I felt towards one another that we had not yet acted upon. I looked at the woman in one of the photographs who had her hands bound behind her back and her eyes blindfolded, and I looked down at Ethan's hands, large and strong, and imagined him holding me tightly like that, binding my arms together, and I felt weak and flushed. He looked at the same photograph and I could hear his breath quicken. Neither of us said anything, and I began to feel even more uncomfortable, and I regretted having mentioned the show to him in the first place. I started moving through the exhibit more quickly, curtailing my urge to spend a long time in front of each frame. With relief we came to the last photograph. On the way out, I leaned towards him a bit, hoping he would touch my elbow or press his arm against mine, but then I realized what I was doing and abruptly pulled away.

The sun was setting as we left, and I was glad for the partial darkness to hide my red face. I was glad, too, that we decided to have dinner in a small restaurant right near the gallery, so I wouldn't have to walk far on my uncertain legs. We ordered wine and dinner, and I was relieved to be sitting and talking, but I still felt uncomfortable because I was so attracted to him. I had not expected this, and I could not account for it. I could remember feeling this way about you. I could recall feeling queasy and weak when I looked at you, but I couldn't tell if this was the same. I thought maybe it was because of the photographs since I had not felt this way when I had seen Ethan in the past. I could not bear that I felt like I wanted to make love with someone else while I could still remember the warmth of your body beside mine, my Aidan.

We had a delicious dinner and drank a bottle of wine. A couple of times while we were talking I felt his knee touch mine under the table, but I pulled away quickly. He walked me home, and when we got to the front door, I knew he was hoping I would invite him in, at least for a drink. Outside the doorway, he turned to me and put his hand on my arm, touched my cheek, and leaned in to kiss me, but stopped himself. I was glad because

I would have enjoyed kissing him back. He looked at me intently, and I knew I would have to say something. *Slowly*, I said. *Not yet*, and *I'm sorry*. He shushed my apology and kissed the back of my hand. I said good night, and went inside. I looked at my hand where he had kissed it and I wanted to press it up against my lips, but I didn't.

Do you remember that photograph of us together at the beginning, when we stood on the bridge? We are holding hands and looking at each other with a ferocious hope. The sun was bright as certainty, and warm as love.

& & &

> And if you can't come into the room without my feeling
> all over me a ripple of flame, & if, wherever you touch me,
> a heart beats under your touch, & if, when you hold me, &
> I don't speak, it's because all the words in me seem to have
> become throbbing pulses, & all my thoughts are a great
> golden blur— why should I be afraid of your smiling at
> me, when I can turn the beads & calico back into such
> beauty— ?
>
> Edith Wharton to W. Morton Fullerton

& & &

In the ocean, I thought. Love would have to be impetuous, saline. Tides, regular and unpredictable, at the mercy of the moon. The sand, churned and battered by every unrelenting wave, settling for only a few hours as the tide abates. Small lives, clams, molluscs, crayfish, transient always, unable to hide beneath the water's assault. How my body might bury itself under the shifting weight of you, further submerged with every wave of your breath. Light and coy as trust, over the surface of the water. Wind pervasive as inconstancy; salt, stinging the skin like a sudden intimacy.

:the way your body never dissolved into mine, fear and longing burning like feet in the sand. How your voice always turned up like the lip of a wave at the end of each sentence, forever hinting at some question:

How love might be in this place. Broken as beached shells, tangled as seaweed. Fluid, astringent words. Amorphous as sand, words arbitrarily pulled like individual grains into the sentence of the sea. Grammar restless as water. I might love you like a boat loves the ocean, buoyant, inextricable, acquiescent, how we are tied to language. Tossed about by its frivolities, at the mercy of its whims. I would wade deep into the water and fill my hands with it the way I did with your words and I would let it run back down into itself until all that was left was a thin film of salt drying in the sun. I would brush this into an envelope and send it to you.

& & &

Aidan was often kind to me. Doing my laundry when I was busy, caring for me when I was ill. He particularly enjoyed giving me massages. Back, temples, legs. My pleasure aroused him. Once, when I had been standing most of the day at the library, he offered to give me a foot rub. He was strong, although a bit rough and clumsy sometimes. He squeezed my heels, pressed smooth lines into my instep, circles on the balls of my feet. Meanwhile we told one another about our respective days, the tedium of work. Distracted, he began pulling my toes, stretching them. I had broken a toe two weeks earlier by stubbing it on a table leg at the library, and when he pulled that one it rebroke, making a sound that reverberated through my skeleton.

Pain like lightning, sharp and ragged as the edge of paper, as doubt.

aphasia [G. speechlessness, fr. *a*- priv. + *phasis*, speech]. Alogia (1); anepia; logagnosia; logamnesia; logasthenia; impaired or absent comprehension of or communication by speech, writing, or signs, due to a dysfunction of brain centers in the dominant hemisphere.

The semaphore of your side. The gestures of your sighs, some nautical language.

Aidan, adrift. Safe at sea.

The sand like so much sorrow.

Rescue me.

An ocean against the dry. This tear a colophon to our story.

Your head against my chest, your hand on my breast, listening as if to a conch shell, some secret language of the sea. To untangle thoughts as though they were seaweed, to move through my language like an eel. Bilingual as a mermaid.

The semantics of saline.

A lingual love, the taste of tears.

Waterlogged words, faith distended, bloated.

Some lighthouse, warning.

An oceanic understanding. How waves converge as they beach themselves, how the pages press in against one another until the words can no longer extricate themselves.

Rescue me, my love.

Bilingual as a mermaid.

Inarticulate as a starfish, the honesty of the exoskeleton. Stiff as grammar.

I would bind your hands with seaweed, I would lick the salt from your skin, I would guide you inside me with short flashes of light, with long beams of light skittering across the water. I would hold you as if I could drown you under me, I would hold you until I felt your tremors, the last spasms of some dying fish. Until I would hear your sigh.

The sound of the sand as it takes the waves into itself.

Aidan, fading, how the cadence of a sentence begins to falter in memory as soon as you close the book.

Bilingual as a mermaid, insistent, inconsistent as the tide.

The aquarium of my body, thick with algae.

Rescue me.

Aidan, asea.

Lingual as.

& & &

(Regret— forked, an arabesque; dissatisfaction spinning, a row of pirouettes. Love as improbable as motionlessness.)

The seat beside me is empty, but in your absence I feel your presence more fully, like the tangibility of the space inscribed by the dancers' arms, rounded, in front of their bodies. *Romeo and Juliet* is onstage, the narrative of another love gone wrong spelled out by the dancers in small perfect gestures, in steps and patterns larger than language. Your ticket, unused, and I console myself with the knowledge that I could not enjoy this through your boredom.

(How few were your acquiescences. The soft bend of the knee as the dancer lands was, to you, a weakness; you had no patience for the way the body concedes to gravity. Agreeing to accompany me to the ballet again is the only surrender I can recall and you have evaded even this. The empty chair mocks; victory yours even in your absence. Inflexibility in the name of strength, the vocabulary of winning and losing in lieu of words of compromise, or understanding. What I wanted was not you, here, beside me (the lie of circumstance), but the act of concession.)

Like love, the dancers' movements seem effortless, limbs precise as the workings of a clock, autonomous but compelled; I am sitting close enough that I can hear the grunts and moans of the dancers, the sighs of relief as they cross the threshold to offstage.

Skin weeping with sweat.

Their movements are measured, prescribed, but it is in the deviations that the true language emerges. The small defiances— an overcurved arm, a penché held a quarter-beat too long, a grimace as the face turns towards the back— the adjectives, adverbs, embellishments that make a language usable. Onstage, they dance this tragedy they can't quite believe in, imagine, with awkward lifts and uncomfortable postures, a love they might die for. Incredulity, longing, in the arch of the foot. Tracing patterns on the stage; rewriting love letters over and over until the pen begins to press through the paper. Covering every inch of the stage. As though love could be scrutinized, explained.

Romeo and Juliet, with everything but their bodies beyond their control, dancing the same steps each night with some small hope that tonight it might end differently, that fate might be eluded. But every night the corps de ballet aligns itself into Capulets and Montagues, distinguishable only by the colour of their costumes, and every night the soloists mime the drinking of the poison and the stabbing of the knife. Every night they surrender to destiny, to the implausibility of love.

And then, tonight, near the end, during one of Romeo and Juliet's pas de deux, Juliet falls. A slipped pointe shoe, a flurry of limbs, both dancers tumbling to the ground, and a sound deep and resonant as wood splitting.

Juliet lies on the stage, clutching her ankle. The music ceases, one instrument at a time, and the dancers drop out of step, out of character, and crowd around her.

(An ankle, fragile as a heart. How I stopped loving you: not with the sharp crack of wood but with slow, silent fissures, invisible at first but growing thick and thorough as veins, so that the break was not a discernible rend but a disintegration, a crumbling. A sudden relenting of the effort of holding it together. And how, in the rubble, I saw the outline of a secret, silent self that I had forgotten about; how I felt, for only one brief moment, triumphant, and I understood your addiction to victory.)

The house doctor runs onto the stage and disappears into the crowd around Juliet. I cannot see, and imagine instead an ankle bent sideways out from her leg, bone piercing the skin, blood running into her white pointe shoe. The incongruity of bone among the soft tights, the reddening satin of her slipper. Audible words on the stage shattering the silent vocabulary of the dance. A plummeting back into the universe of words, and I refuse to understand them, there is only the expression of pain I imagine on her face. The curtain begins to lower and a voice asks us to wait while the understudy warms up to complete the ballet. I can hear only the crack of ankle through the announcer's words, and I can't bear to watch a new Juliet, so I push my way out past the other patrons and leave the theatre.

(How, a week before I could articulate the end of our love, I saw a baby squirrel hit by a car. It was silent, insignificant, and the driver probably never knew he hit anything: just another small tragedy. Tire over hips, and the squirrel hesitated before screeching, careening across the street sideways, bent in half.

The pure sound of agony, of imminent death. The shriek, silent, in my throat; the shape of your name.)

As I walk out of the theatre I try to push from my mind the sound of the ankle breaking, the sight of the squirrel; these remind me of the last time we were in the same room. Boxes everywhere, the detritus of broken hope. We argued over the ownership of books, CDs, photographs; we cried and held one another. One of us had to be the first to walk out the door; I can't remember who.

And then I imagine the next time I will see you. How I will have to talk you as if you were just anybody else, how I will have to push the sound of your sobs from my mind if I am not to cry myself. How I will have to pretend not to know everything about you; how I will have to stop myself from touching you without even thinking about it. How you may have a new shirt, a different haircut, new pieces of you I won't know. How the divergence of our lives will be reflected in your eyes.

(The inadequate language of the body. The mime of sorrow. No words for resolve or relief or regret.

The impossibility of remembering the forgotten, of forgetting the indelible. To shed language like the memory of long-ago ballet steps; to erase every book in the library; to lose the words of you.)

aphonia [G. *a-* priv. + *phone,* voice]. Anaudia; loss of the voice as a result of disease or injury of organ of speech.

Another draft— the language still too imprecise. I collect the pages of it and tear them into pieces, a sound like waves collapsing on the shore. Dozens of slips of paper; a letter, a word, a paragraph, white. I take the largest fragment to the poetry section. I find a book that has one of your poems in it and I put the piece of paper there, flush with the top of the pages, *ome lighthouse warni / oceanic understandin* laid across your words. And then the smallest piece, *escue m,* I take to the reference section and put it in the medical dictionary, marking Hemophilia B (Christmas Disease). And then the other jagged pieces, in random order. Putting each in a different book, some chosen because they are important to me, some because they are not, and some for no reason at all.

And then, disembowelled and hidden, buttressed by my library, the words begin to mean what I want them to; my letter, emerging.

& & &

In the forest, where love has to be luminous, solid. Trees thick as promises, green as disillusion. Wind, cool, soft, moist, winding itself in around thick trunks, how I wrap myself around your body in the night, how the breath of your words weaves itself in through my pores. And when the wind stills, then the leaves rest against one another, letters leaning into some sentence, sounds of waiting. Leaves soft as skin, trunks rough and solid as fear.

:the way honesty weaves itself through, around, against our narrative, how we believed in it, clear as the sky:

How love is in this place. Lush as language, moist as a tongue. Fertile as adjectives. Movement stilled, a path too convoluted for verbs. Here we might find peace, we might love more slowly. Where sound is drawn out, sustained. With the thoroughness of undergrowth, the defiance of the evergreen. Chronicled by the rings of the trees, damped by a cushion of decaying leaves. I will press a leaf into my book, the way you pressed me into you.

& & &

The syntax of lips, the grammar of a kiss. I had thought, Aidan, when I kissed Ethan it would be incomprehensible; instead it was as familiar as my own words.

We met for a drink, Ethan and I, in a quiet bar. We had a

corner to ourselves, and I was uncomfortable because it seemed so ostentatiously romantic. I felt as though there were no way to escape this, as though a relationship had somehow become inevitable in spite of my indecision. I enjoyed the way I could talk with him. Ethan kept leaning forward, almost as if he could capture more of my breath, my words, if he were nearer. At one point he moved his hand across the table toward mine. I started discernibly, and dropped my hand under the table onto my lap. He frowned and looked exasperated. I had sensed his impatience the last time we had been out, and I had felt indignant because he had no right to me, and at the same time a bit guilty, as though I were leading him on. I had to force myself not to apologize about my hand. Instead I changed the subject, but he continued to sulk for some time, and after we finished our drinks, he suggested we leave. By this time, I was feeling angry at his petulance, but at the same time angry with myself for upsetting him. He walked me home again, and before I knew what I was saying, I had invited him in for tea. He brightened at this, and I felt better.

He came in for tea, and we talked for a long time, until early in the morning. Finally, after saying several times that he had to leave but not actually doing it, he put his shoes on and got up to go. I walked him to the door, and, again without thinking about it, I reached up and kissed him on the lips. As I pulled away, I looked at his startled eyes, and I tried to decide if I had done that because I wanted to or because I was afraid of disappointing him again. I could not make up my mind which it was. His lips were warm and soft, and after he looked for a long time into my eyes, he kissed me back, long and full. I felt my lungs shrink, as if I couldn't get any air, and I felt his tongue reach out for mine. His kisses were exquisite, dexterous and subtle, and I felt my body strain toward his. His arms went tight around me and I felt his hands touch my sides where the rib begins to curve. This made me want him, and I had to muster all my strength to tell him to stop. He sighed and mumbled, but good-humouredly, and he left with only a little protest. As I heard his steps down the hall, I locked the door and stared at it for some time, trying to understand what I had done. How could I want this and not want this so emphatically at the same time? There was no trace of you, Aidan, in his taste or the shape of his kisses. How will I find you again, if not there? And how will I lose you if I look for you there?

An alphabet of loss, a language of tongues. The indeterminate vocabulary of kisses.

& & &

Whenever we would drive past a cow pasture, my father would stop the car and stick his head out the window to moo at the cows. They would look up from their grazing and come to the fence by the car and stare. I would laugh, delighted, and then, when I was a little older, look away embarrassed, impatient.

(To write to you this way: loudly, certainly, with abandon and with pleasure. To risk making an ass of myself by speaking, ineloquently, in your language.)

& & &

I saw your friend today. At first he pretended not to see me, but when he couldn't avoid me, he smiled widely and quickly hugged me. When I looked at his face, I could only see it as it looked just before he kissed me, and so it was difficult to talk to him. He explained how busy he'd been, how sorry he was that he hadn't been able to call me. He said, too, that he'd been looking forward to seeing me. As he said these things that I knew were lies, I remembered my hands holding his face and his hair tangled on the pillow, and in his words I could hear his moans. I shifted my legs to disperse the warmth I could feel there. I was angry with myself for feeling aroused by his presence and for allowing myself to feel hurt by his rejection, and, of course, I was angry with him. I did not want him to see how I felt, didn't want him to know he could affect me. So I feigned nonchalance, and, like him, talked only of inconsequential matters. I could have loved you, I wanted to say, but I didn't. I was ashamed that I cared about it. I kept looking at the inside of his arm, thinking how soft it was and how I wanted to touch it. I knew, too, that he wanted to ask me if I had told you about us, but was afraid to bring up the subject at all in case I asked him more about it. Our trivial conversation went on for a short while, and then he said he had to hurry off to a meeting. I suspected that this, like much of what he had said, was untrue, but I was relieved to be done talking. He assured me he would call soon, and we could plan to go out, and I nodded. I watched him walk away and I felt so foolish and humiliated that I had believed that I had meant something to him in the first place, and that I could feel myself wanting to believe him again. I resolved again to not think about him, and to not expect anything further from him, but still I felt hopeful, and ashamed for it, although in truth I did not care so much for him. I knew I would never love him, that I only wanted him to want me because in some way it was as if you wanted me again. And so I was hurt by his rejection because it was your rejection all over again. I was more ashamed about that than anything else.

& & &

Your eyes, left to right, left to right, down a little each time, zigzagging a bit when your attention would wane; I would, sometimes, watch you read. I would imagine the words as your gaze passed over them, which words might slow your eyes down, send them back over the last few lines either in admiration or confusion, what kind of sentence you might gloss over. I wanted to know how you understood what you read, how the moments that awed you might influence your own writing. I would think of your recent poems and look for signs of the books you were reading as you wrote them, images, moods, turns of phrase that might echo these books.

(Words like the filigree of a spider's web, and I try to trace it backwards, round and round towards a centre that is both beginning and end.)

aporia [G. *aporia*, difficulty, doubt]. Doubt, especially deriving from incompatible views on the same subject.

Aidan, this evening I am going to him, to Ethan. (The way the sound of your name is refracted inside his.) You, again, always; after this I will have to remember you differently. The relentlessness of this ending, the way it is always beginning again.

It's raining, and the impatience, the directness, of the dark rain drowns out my hesitation. I knock lightly on his door, he opens it, takes my wet coat from my shoulders. I am slow through the doorway, startled by dryness, by his warmth, by the sudden fear, pleasure, that when I look at him naked he will not have the same soft skin, the same red hairs as you, Aidan. Will he know I look for figures of you in the shadows his arm casts along his side, will he know that as I run my fingers across his skin I will be trying to discern the shape of you beneath?

While I am still near the entrance to his apartment he takes my shoulders and pulls me to him. Fingers like breath across my cheeks, his face drawing nearer to me. Such a soft, slow kiss, long and languorous, and we fall against the wall. Desire sharp as pain.

I gasp so deeply I feel my collapsed lungs grow and split, the taste of that breath unfamiliar, and I feel it ease itself in around the centre of you. His tongue in my throat like a foreign language; we slide slowly down the wall. And I pull at his shirt and I feel the hard hull of his ribs, I lay my fingers between them as if to make him solid. He takes his shirt off, slowly, and I lay both my hands against his chest and I run my hands up and down the shape of him. The bliss of nipples against my tongue. He removes my shirt, my pants, impatient at the incongruity of cloth among this flesh. And he stands me up with his tongue, so sweet between my thighs, his fingers pulling on my nipples, towards him. And then he is smiling at me and he carries me to his bed and there we taste each other, slowly, all over, tongues painting a new vocabulary. The sweet saltiness of sweat, a taste of feral blood, and I suck him, as if I might draw some of this beauty through him and into me. And now I am writhing, I beg him *now now please now inside me* and he lays me on my back and hovers over me *ask again* and *now now I'll die without* as I feel this sudden hollowness inside me as though I have been torn open. And he enters me, gently at first while I become accustomed to his foreignness and then harder, faster, until the bed begins to dance over the floor, so hard I feel him in the centre of every cell. So hard, as if he could push the memory of you out through my pores. And when I think this I realize you are nowhere here except this thought, I did not feel the *not you* when he pushed inside me, I forgot to notice that his lips are not yours, and I'm sad because I'm not sure I have wrung everything from this sorrow as it ebbs and I'm relieved because I don't want Ethan to doubt me, because the sanctity of touch has reasserted itself. And when he comes, you are gone, Aidan, there is only this coming. We collapse into sleep the way I collapsed around the pain of you and there is some newness to this, it is the harbinger of some future sorrow, and my last thought before sleep is of you, of the sadness of you.

& & &

For all that lies
between the barrenness of
memory and this palpable grief,
neither noun nor verb nor adjective,
one word,
a collusion of these,
describing that place
between hope and
cruelty, love
and abasement,
circumscribing metaphor and bliss,
absence and metonymy.

A word that lies quietly
in the spaces
between these letters,
vestigial,
in invisible ink
legible only through the heat of
sorrow, or wrath,
or despair.

aprosexia [G. *a*- priv. + *prosexis,* attention, fr. *pros-echo,* to hold to]. Inattention, due to a sensorineural or mental defect.

When we were caught in that sudden rainstorm one summer evening; the wind came up so suddenly and wrapped our hair around each other's faces and I could taste the redness of you, and then the rain splashed down so hard and so fast. Gravity couldn't keep up, the streets began to flood because the water wouldn't rush down into the gutters fast enough, and we were wading down the sidewalk, my dress vulnerable, transparent against my legs. Everyone was laughing, the audacity of the rain surprising everyone into happiness. But I grumbled a bit, soured, complained of the empty chill left in the vacuum after the rain.

Heartrending, this violation. The smile slowly left your face, and we walked on in silence.

The language of rain: an almost silent patter, the individual drops indiscernible, inarticulable. The particular cadence of rain, how the sound surrounds you like skin, like love. The different dialects as it hits the pavement, the grass, a certain roof, all as familiar to my ear as your whisper. As though the rain is in communication with all the water in my body, the way the body is more supple in the rain, more dangerous. I would send you the rain as my letter, a torrent, a light mist, large round drops; the ways I have loved you.

& & &

Hemophilia B: aphasia of the blood. Forgetting how to clot itself into words. Instead, its muffled, wordless screams rising to the surface in bruises, the stuttering, pooling of sounds, of warmth and pain, in the joints, the inarticulate escapes, unstoppable, through the skin. The syllables of symptoms amassed into one word only in middle age: the sudden mortality of my father.

(*Christmas disease, hmpphhh,* he would joke. *Some lousy present.* And *If it's good enough for the tsars of Russia, then it's good enough for me. With my blood Russian out my arm, heh heh.*)

Normal coagulation processes disrupted: blood mumbling, lisping, rambling. Not only on the outside, red spurting, sheeting, but on the inside, too, easing itself through muscles, joints, soft tissue. The way the letters on a page of type blur when wet, ink with a mind of its own, refusing to be contained by its font, its arteries. Blood loss, nerve damage, muscle deterioration, osteoarthritis: the dialect of the hemophiliac body.

The treatment for Christmas disease is the infusion of factor

IX concentrates, manufactured or drawn from donated blood, like injecting consonants into the aphasic's stream of vowels until words solidify. But these concentrates have other proteins that work too well, causing thrombosis— the way a word with too many consonants thickens, halts. The irony of a hemophiliac dying from a blood clot.

That he knew this would probably happen was no preparation. The shock that something so permanent as death could be so spontaneous. So ordinary. The startling inefficacy of pleading, of bargaining, of prayer or hope. I watched the onslaught of death with him, he held my hand and we saw it approach and then all at once I knew I was watching alone. A sudden articulateness of blood; a new vocabulary of stillness and loss and grief.

& & &

I woke up this morning in Ethan's bed and I was relieved I had to get up to go to work. I am afraid of a leisurely morning with him— of lying naked in the brightness, talking and smiling and touching. I did not want him to watch me eat my breakfast, I did not want to have any picture of morning but the one you and I shared, Aidan. The brand of orange juice you like, the way you butter your toast, how your hair looks mussed, pillow lines on your face; I don't want morning to be anything but that. I didn't want Ethan to see my sleepy face, my unbrushed teeth, because these things are still yours.

I did not sleep well, although Ethan did. I tossed and turned, feeling the unfamiliar texture of his sheets, and it made me remember your skin. I lay there all night thinking about these things, and how I love you and how I don't love you, and how I hate you and how I don't, and worrying that I couldn't remember the first morning I spent with you. And I breathed in the smell of Ethan and I liked it and every time I would fall asleep for a little while I would awaken to find myself curled tightly around him.

(The contagious warmth of skin, the slow swell of memory.)

At the library I was unable to concentrate, and I kept alphabetizing the same pile of books again and again because I couldn't remember the order of the letters. Every time I ran my fingers down the pile I would think of Ethan curled up beside me, the knobs of his spine against my body, and I would feel a flush through my hips and across my thighs. All day I felt pages rustling inside me.

(I hadn't wanted to want him.)

I tried to think about the books I was returning to the shelves. The constancy of the alphabet, the sound of the books sliding, snug, into their allotted places; these acts of completion in place of longing. But I kept thinking about lying next to Ethan, and about lying next to you, Aidan, and I couldn't remember the first morning I spent with you, and I was still trying to shelve the books and I began to imagine that there was not one alphabet, but two. With two there would be enough letters for words to say everything I want to say to both of you, and then this would be done.

(The sun was bright and it came, strong and white through your window, shining across our bodies. I could feel it through my eyelids before I saw it, and when I opened my eyes I was momentarily blinded. In the same way, I could feel your body, Aidan, beside me as I was coming up through sleep and I felt so happy before I knew why. You were still asleep, and I lay beside you, feeling your slow breath, and then I felt your body come awake, and we lay beside each other, wordless, for some time. Then we began to talk, bright and sweet and warm, and when we talked about a song you sat up a bit and you sang it to me, clear as the light. And then the sun began to relent, and I felt a bit sad, and I knew that had been a perfect time, and it would never come again.)

& & &

I would love you in a marsh. Fetid, submerged. Water, dark and viscous; the air, expectant. The stench of stillness, punctuated by the sharp ellipsis of bird cries, the rumble of frogs. Unstoppable growth choking the water. I would pull up handfuls of mud, of algae; you would feel them, silky on your palms, and this would be my letter.

& & &

Sometimes my father and mother would yell at each other so loudly that the sounds didn't seem to be composed of words any more. Anger flashing like light off steel, and then quiet— a surrender, a resolution, or a departure.

(To write to you this way, with gesture and volume in place of meaning, a sudden hush.)

& & &

During the day, thinking about my night with Ethan and about my letter to you, I misshelved several books. I sorted them incorrectly on the cart, mixing reference and poetry, history and fiction. I caught my error partway through shelving and went back and moved the books to their proper places, except for one of my favourite novels, which I left in the languages section.

When I got home I could still feel the quiver of exhilaration when I thought of my revolt. I looked at my own bookcases, alphabetized, if not arranged by call number, and I felt embarrassed by my orderliness, caged in by it. I took all the books with

A authors off the shelf and redistributed them throughout the alphabet. Then I took one shelf, with the *H* authors on it, and rearranged it so it was in alphabetical order by title rather than author.

To shuffle my alphabet like a shelf of books, finding in this defiance a new language for my letter; atoms realigning until a precipitate suddenly emerges, like meaning.

aprosody [G. *a-* priv. + *prosodia,* voice modulation].
Absence, in speech, of the normal pitch, rhythm, and
variations in stress.

Soft as a vowel, your tongue;
the hard assonance of your absence.

(I would spell this longing onto your back,
the vocabularies of fingertips and nails.)

The sentience, sentence of my
flesh, incomplete;
no verb in your absence.

The stillness of the subject,
the slowness of a night without you.

The way my voice rises
into a question.

The restraints of grammar, how you would
tie my hands to the headboard.

A series of clauses, a catalogue of losses, a
catastrophic motionlessness.

(I would write deep bruises onto your shoulder, makeshift
punctuation for an inopportune conversation.)

Lingering, like some unfinished word.

How the phonemes, across your tongue, might
align themselves into meaning, how
your body might press itself against me,
some perfect phrase.

& & &

Once, early night, we lay in a bed away from home; a velvet stillness, a perfect dark. We lay side by side holding hands, and then you leaned up on one elbow and kissed me. Softly, quietly, lips unstrained and tender. We kissed for a long time, like we never did at home any more. Our kisses were tender, too, instead of hurried and demanding. We began touching one another, gently, thoroughly, lingering on all the places we were usually impatient with— forearms, necks, stomachs. All the while we talked and giggled into each other's mouths, *oh no, we shouldn't* and *stop, stop, they'll hear us.*

And then you quietly eased yourself on top of me and entered me. We moved slowly, entirely in unison, to keep the bed from squeaking. Thrusting so soft and tender it was excruciating, a perfect rhythm, and we kept forgetting to breathe. Fighting the urge for faster, deeper, louder, more, we moved silently together until, before we realized what was about to happen, we both came, our hands over each other's mouths to stifle the moans. You shuddered and lay on top of me for a while, trying to catch your breath without making any noise. We curled up together for sleep.

And then I realized I was crying, lines of tears across my face. You saw, too, and apologized again and again, certain you had hurt me during our lovemaking. I could not make you understand that you had not, that I was crying for some inexplicable reason, for the perfection of that moment, for the inevitable arc of love. A sadness like I had never felt passed over me— irrational, prophetic, unassailable— and I had to give in to you, pretend I felt some physical pain that would soon pass to comfort you.

& & &

I was showing someone how to use the computer when Ethan walked into the library this afternoon. I had known he would either call or show up because I had left in such a hurry in the morning, but I was still flustered when he arrived. I gestured to him to wait and continued to give instructions on doing a title search, although I had pretty much exhausted the subject. I needed a few minutes to compose myself. I could feel my face turning a deep red, and the man I was helping looked at me oddly, because I was so addled and because I had repeated my entire explanation twice over. He thanked me emphatically at the end of my second run through the instructions and hurried away. I still didn't feel calm, but I walked over to where Ethan was waiting. I didn't know if he was expecting a kiss, but my co-workers were already staring because he had brought me a rose. I was also flustered because I felt I was undeserving and I was still uncertain, although at the same time I wanted to wrap my arms around him. I agreed to go to a film with him. I am apprehensive about this because I don't have to work tomorrow and will have no excuse to leave in the morning, but although I had the chance to refuse graciously, I did not.

(There is no room for this in my letter to you, Aidan. How will I find words for it that are not words of you?)

& & &

Sails, the wind's skin; a vertebral mast. We sit inside the boat as if we might find respite there, as if there were such a thing as sanctuary. Adrift upon the horizon, we might love differently here. The sea, impenetrable, we skitter across its surface; the rhythmic slap of waves to lull us into desire. I sit low in the boat, at the bow, and watch where we have been, the shoreline a sentence in some foreign language. I sit, still, and run my fingers along the inside of the hull again and again, feeling as though I were you, inside my own body. It makes me want to touch you, and I reach across and run my hand up your arm, like a rib of the boat. I tell you how the boat is like a body, and how the movement of the water makes me imagine how you feel when you are inside me, and it makes me want you. You nod, but don't seem to be listening, and you pull a bit harder on the ropes, as if the wind were your marionette. As though the wind were predictable, constant, faithful; as though love, like wood, were buoyant. As if words could be rudders, setting a course for us to some perfect island. As if water could be, for even a moment, motionless.

& & &

Eclipse
for Ethan

First touch, drops of blood from some sun. Fingertips on my thigh, a constellation, a consolation. A moon ripe as fear, vast as intentions. Banal as a love poem.

Such omens; I avert my eyes. An insufferable weakness. Inadequacy beading, some dew forecasting dawn.

I would write to you that I feel the presence of you swelling in me, an autumn plum. I would write to you that your absence presses into my skin like dampness, that I feel fear, thick as bone, as night, in my empty bed.

(If I did not have to hear the scratch of the pen, if I did not have to see your eyes dart across the words. If I thought the way the reflection of the moon skitters across the water were not a lie, if I thought the stars stayed bright during an eclipse.)

& & &

My door has not been opened once today, but what my
heart palpitated. There were moments when I feared to
hear your voice, and then I was disconsolate that it was not
your voice. So many contradictions, so many contrary
movements are true, and can be explained in three words:
I love you.

Julie-Jeanne-Eléonore de l'Espinasse to the
Comte de Guibert

& & &

I have catalogued your cruelties.
They lie, fetid, in the pores of language's skin,
swelling and festering—
I worry them to the surface with a fingernail,
pull at them to yield.
(The pustulence of meaning, fertile only beneath this.)

:what you said at the end. that we had been young and foolish, that our love had been a game, play-acting. that you had been meaning to end it for some time, and simply hadn't bothered. that it had long been a burden to you. how you let me fear all along that our love was much more important to me than it was to you. how you fucked me even when I didn't want you to, because somehow I thought I owed it to you, and how you made me feel like my body wasn't mine:

The resolute kinship of love and cruelty,
how knowledge and gentleness are irreconcilable,
how the fingers can arc and separate, an infinite vocabulary.

apyrexia [G. *a-* priv. + *pyrexis*, fever]. Absence of fever.

With the pages, the chapters, in the wrong order; with the spine on the right side of the page instead of the left; upside-down; with the wrong cover, the wrong title; on both sides, the book sealed shut:

:the ways that binding a book, like love, can go wrong.

& & &

On a glacier. Where love is slow, determined, impenetrable. Solid and dense as ice. A piercing cold. The omnivorous glare of sunlight from above and below, unrelenting as your faithlessness, sharp as your voice. Ice, impervious to the heat of the sun, only the surface succumbs to its warmth, a thin sheen of water across the ice. Treacherous as your soft words. Small plants and stones frozen deep into the ice beneath us, specks of meaning glimmering up through the vastness of congealed words.

:the way a glacier moves, with certainty and patience and

imperviousness; how your doubt pressed itself over us, slowly, deliberately, the soft sun of longing futile against this cold:

Love in this place: slow and irrelevant as adverbs, solid as nouns. Words clear and sure. Here we would have loved more immensely, like a paragraph. Meaning frozen unequivocally into words, weighty and ineluctable. Ink dark and irrefutable as midnight ice, I would have spoken with enormity and inevitability. I will chisel off bits of ice and place them in an envelope; they will melt into your hand, and this will be my letter to you.

& & &

The Christmas I was almost two, my parents bought me a small plastic barn, with small plastic animals and farm people and a small plastic tractor. The joy of surprise, of unwrapping, of ownership. When the barn door opened, it made a loud mooing sound. I closed the door quickly and reopened it. It mooed again. I was terrified by this sound. My father grabbed the barn, ran to the basement, and disconnected the noise.

(To write a letter that would ease the noise in my head, a letter that would bring safety and protection.)

& & &

All through the movie I could feel Ethan's leg beside mine. I didn't pay much attention to the film because I was thinking about this unfamiliar thigh and remembering the feel of it, naked, against mine in the night, and about how different it was from yours, Aidan, firmer and with more hair. I was trying to visualize your legs but I could only see them like a photograph, textureless and unreal. This failure of memory disturbs me. It suggests that I didn't love you well enough to remember, or that it is so important to me that I have no choice but to forget.

As I thought about this, I reached across and put my hand on Ethan's thigh, partly because I wanted to remember yours and partly because I wanted to touch him. He was engrossed in the film, but broke his concentration long enough to cover my hand with his, and tuck his fingertips under my palm. It was similar to a gesture you used to make, a sort of absentminded hand-holding. I remember the weight of your large hand, the suffocation, and how our hands would begin to sweat. You would always let go and wipe your palm on your pants; I was always disappointed, although I, too, felt hot and uncomfortable.

After the film ended, Ethan waited patiently through the credits because I made no move to get up. I was trying to decide what to do next, although I knew I would go over to his place and we would make love again. I was sad, thinking about you and about holding hands with you, and at the same time, I felt a bit defiant, as though I should let myself want Ethan to spite you. I was dismayed to be thinking this, and to be thinking about you, when I should have been thinking about what it was I wanted and why I was afraid. This subject seemed too enormous for the short time the credits would take to roll, however, and I let my mind be made up by the sudden memory of the times I left movies halfway through because you wanted to and I was too afraid of your disapproval to refuse. This thought, ludicrous as it was, made me stay through to the end of the credits and made me decide to go home with Ethan. He had moved his leg away as the credits started, as if he had known what I was thinking, and I suddenly missed its warmth.

& & &

I would love you in a labyrinth. Hedges high as hope, green as fear. I begin at the entrance, collecting the breadcrumbs of the last to leave, wending my way into the cacophony of leaves until at last I find myself deep at the centre, irretrievably lost. I press the breadcrumbs together in my palm: my letter.

& & &

In the darkroom, I imagine, making prints of you and me together. Red, like an artery; the movement of fluid in the trays. Us, standing outside your parents' house. At first I underexpose the print, quieting the black, bleaching out the happiness on our faces. I adjust the time, leave the next print too long under the enlarger, light burning itself into black, and then there is only darkness, premonitory. And when I get the time right for the third print and I slide it into the tray of developer, I watch your face slowly emerge from the white, underwater, otherworldly. I move it to the stop bath, the fixer, and then I leave it to rinse, your face bobbing and sinking, bending under the moving water.

My letter: translucent as film, bright as the searing light of the enlarger, a progression of fluids. I write shapes and lines onto paper with light, with a vocabulary of only whites and blacks and greys. Figures of love, and loss: an alphabet of texture and contour.

arrhythmia [G. *a-* priv. + *rhythmos,* rhythm]. Loss of rhythm; denoting especially an irregularity of the heartbeat.

I found a draft of one of your poems, Aidan, in among my papers. I began to read it and realized that I still knew it, that I could anticipate what words would come next. And I realized, too, quite suddenly, that I didn't like it. That, if I were to be honest, I didn't really like any of your poetry, although it was much of what drew me to you in the first place. I read the poem again, trying to pretend it was someone else's poem in case I only disliked it out of some resentment towards you, but I still felt the same way.

I will cut all your poems into their individual words, the way my body has been desiccated by the absence of your touch. I will rearrange them and address them back to you.

& & &

The taste of blood, hot and salty, benign. Would my father have tasted its disease, its treacherousness?

(To write to you with the taste of death's imminence skulking through the ink, the spectre of ending tangled through.)

& & &

> Of all wretched women I am the most wretched, and amongst the unhappy I am unhappiest. The higher I was exalted when you preferred me above all other women, the greater my suffering over my own fall and yours, when I was flung down; for the higher the ascent, the heavier the fall. Has Fortune ever set any great or noble woman over me or made her my equal, only to be similarly cast down and crushed with grief? What glory she gave me in you, what ruin she brought upon me through you! Violent in either extreme, she showed no moderation in good or evil. To make me the saddest of all women she first made me blessed above all, so that when I thought how much I had lost, my consuming grief would match my crushing loss, and my sorrow for what was taken from me would be the greater for the fuller joy of possession which had gone

> before; and so that the happiness of supreme ecstasy would end in the supreme bitterness of sorrow.
>
> Eloïse to Abelard

& & &

Paragraphs like bodies. Piled on library shelves: a mass grave. With a pen I write a new skin for them, adorn them. Hide them. Disarm the white space that is doubt. Comments, explications, reactions, synonyms, trivialities, irrelevancies— horizontally, vertically, diagonally across the margins. Sometimes I add words to the sentences already there, embellish them; sometimes I use the margins as if they were my journal, my letter.

(I had never written in a library book before. Transgression, trespass, the thrill of violation.)

I do this surreptitiously, smuggle books home from work with me. With a black pen I mimic their fonts, with blue I use only script. Red, green, purple ink: neat block letters, illustrations, tiny chickenscratch, sprawling print. Penmanship inconsistent as language. Inconsiderate and invasive as our love. Territorial as fear.

& & &

I would sculpt you this letter, smooth stone in place of my shapeless words. A thick block of alabaster, all my words of you compressed and fossilized, and hiding inside is the perfect letter. I see the shape of it through the mass of dense white, as I prepare my tools. With each one I imagine how it brings my perfect letter nearer into focus, seeing not the shape I will unearth but the shape of what I will take away. The words that shatter, fall to the floor with each tap of the mallet. The boucharde, to soften the stone, fissures forming between syllables; the pitcher, entire vocabularies in alabaster surrendering. My chisel, points, claw, uncovering this perfect shape, both round and angular, sharp and gentle. And finally, files and rifflers to shave away the last impotent phonemes complicating and obscuring my words to you.

And then it would be done. I would have it always, to run my fingers over on some bright morning, a touchstone of grief, and I would remember the smoothness of you.

& & &

I have stopped saying your name aloud. Sometimes I try to use it but when I reach for it I can't find it, because there can't be one word that is you. And sometimes it comes up to my lips and I seal them tight to keep it from escaping. As though there were some finite amount of the sound of you, that every time I speak your name I lose a little more of you.

& & &

I find remembrances of you on my body in these ways.

My hand curves towards a fist; in the shape of it I see how my fingers wove into yours, holding hands until the damp slicked into wet and we let go.

A raised scar, white, thick with the presence, the absence of you.

How my nipples stiffen in the cold, hardening themselves into the shape of the hollow inside your mouth.

Five long bruises around my arm, your fingerprints discernible in the yellow.

I tilt my head to one side, feel the warmth of my naked shoulder, and just for a minute I think this perfect, cradling warmth is yours.

The faint memory of a long-ago bruise on my thigh, where your hipbone would rest.

How my feet look for yours in the night.

A tickle on my palm like the flutter of your eyelashes.

I bump into the corner of a table; it is the sharpness of your elbow.

The pulse of music, how I would hold my ear to your chest; a heartbeat, the rush of blood like a conch shell.

This is how I remember you: a phantom limb.

asyndesis [G. *a-* priv. + *syn*, together, + *desis*, binding]. **1.** A mental defect in which separate ideas or thoughts cannot be joined into a coherent concept. **2.** A breaking up of the connecting links in language, said to be characteristic of language disturbance of schizophrenics.

I am out with Ethan, we are riding on his motorcycle through the countryside. It is autumn, the leaves are turning, fickle, and the heat of summer is beginning to capitulate. The quiver of uneven roads through our bodies, flesh fluttering like drying leaves, my arms tight around his waist. I let go and set my hands firmly on his thighs, I can feel the violence of the engine through him, the disturbance of bones. I run my hands slowly up between his thighs. We stop the bike and walk into the woods.

Until I am leaning into a tree, arms, the back of my head pressed into the bark the way he is pressed into me. And he gasps louder and louder, the air catching on some jagged word as he exhales, and I breathe his sounds back into his mouth, and then we moan and hold each other tighter, fingernails pushing into flesh, until

And then you, Aidan. The emptiness between the ridges of bark, the awkwardness of limbs shooting off from the trunk. And then I am sobbing, crouched under this tree of you, my pants locking around my ankles, bark imprinting itself onto my vertebrae. You, always you, only where I never expect to find you.

& & &

I would love you in a river. The futility of water, its unceasing movement. Impotent against the shore; how it chisels away at its own bed. The density of mud, the clarity of water. How it pushes itself over the banks in spring. Minnows flashing by like happiness.

& & &

Once I saw my father hit his thumb with a hammer, hard. He swore, sharply, then long and low, until his curses became his breath.

(To have a vocabulary so eloquent about pain, to have language merge with breath, to write this as an exhalation, instinctive.)

& & &

In a garden, I thought. Love is fecund, idyllic. Leaves, the pages of some new, verdant language, flowers bright as lust. The smell of black loam; here love might breathe deeply. The recurrence of morning; the assuredness of dew. A smothering hope; it is enough in place of an inadequate love. An opulence of colour to disguise our monochromatic faith. Here love obeys the seasons— the strangling growth of summer, the irrefutability of autumn, of brown and of decay. We might practise prudence then, leaves sere as paper, the dryness of even the air. The patience of winter, the inevitability of spring, its explosion.

:the way roots grow, inextricable and searching, how we might have loved one another enough. Doubt and fear like a drought, and first the edges of the leaves begin to wither into brown, and:

How love is in this place. We learn words like new buds, they flower into sentences perfect with meaning. Every paragraph of land distinctive. Soil fertile as nouns, adjectives like so many shades of green. Verbs articulate as the movements of leaves in the wind, adverbs plentiful as the different patterns of sunlight on petals. Conjunctions superfluous as weeds in this profusion of colour. Here, in this excess, we find the words for our love, here we might have talked of sustenance, of longevity and fertility. I will pick all the brightest flowers and press them between my palms until they dry, bright and flat as paper, and I will place them in an envelope; when you open it this garden will fall into your hands and this will be my letter to you.

& & &

Blood, treacherous as love.

To rewrite the ending of my father's story, to defer it, or make it tidier, or slower, or gentler. To make it mine. To make him have told me he loved me or to make me not have looked away at the end. To make it have happened at home. To make it slower, less ordinary. To take away my father's pain, to take away mine. To add flourishes that would make the story uniquely my father's, a joke, a gesture, a word that would make it not just another small tragedy.

To make not every love be this love; to make not every ending be this ending.

& & &

Unspoken phonemes coagulating under my skin, dense and blackening. A clot of words; if I could write this with words sharp as scalpels I might scrape it from beneath my skin. The dexterity of verbs, the sureness of nouns, the sentence they might slice into my skin. Blood escapes the cut, the predictability of prepositions, it thins and spreads, as diffuse as adjectives. I ply the skin apart, the angry red of unexposed words, and from this wetness I pull all the words of my perfect letter in strings of flesh. I lay them in a steel dish and they begin to dry in the sterile air, turning black like ink, and I smell the stench of their malignance. With thread thin as silence I begin to write small, fine stitches, pulling this incision together, and when it heals I remove the thread. I put it in an envelope and when you open it, it falls into the shape of my words to you.

& & &

One match. To choose one page from one book, any of a million pages, and to touch the match to its corner or its middle or a single word. And then watching the red, spreading across the paper to the next and then the next until the whole library is suffocating in smoke. Flame, uncompromising and undiscriminating, word by word, book by book, through the stacks. The futility of the sprinkler, of language, against this.

Splinters of spines, of covers. Ash, wet and dark as ink. I gather a handful; this is my letter.

& & &

Dawn unfurling.

(Words like
parentheses
around what I would tell you.)

The stutter of
light,
dark's ellipsis through morning.

(My impatience at
commas. The
tyranny of want and of unspoken
words.)

The multiplication of sun
through a drop of dew,
how you inscribe light on paper,
breath on a neck.

avulsion [L. *a-vello*, pp. *-vulsus*, to tear away]. A tearing away or forcible separation.

Desire tight like skin.

The reckless teleology of want, gestures like one-way streets.

Words like blades, and I was aroused by your cruelty.

The humiliation of not being loved enough. (A disdainful touch, and I opened my legs to you.)

I would have had you beat me, whip me, I would have had you brand me. A tangible possessiveness, a written love: I would have had you want to make me yours. Love enough for hurtfulness. I would have had you bind me that I might know you wanted to keep me near. To slap my cheek, a print of you upon my face that you might be closer; to punch my chest that I might breathe you in more deeply. The blue of bruises, your inky signature.

A labyrinthine obsession.

& & &

A word that I wanted to say to you at the corner of a page: I tear it off. And then another word, in a different book, in the middle of the page: I tear the whole page out. Every day, to find the word I want to say to you. A pile on my desk, corners, half-pages, whole leaves, all in different textures, colours, different fonts. A pile of incongruous words, linked by transgression, by you. A cacophony, a silence: my letter.

& & &

I would love you in fire. Red and orange and yellow, as inconstant as we are. The impermanence of fuel, the clumsiness of flame. Unrelenting heat; how we distrusted apology and forgiveness. A searing hope, the inevitability of ash, smouldering like dissent. A palpable blackness.

& & &

The shapes of words like unfamiliar bodies across the page. The evaporation of meaning; a sudden foreignness of the anatomy of language. I look at my words to you again and they are only shapes. The notation for some perfect choreography, a ballet in ink. I read the dance there, the motions of the first and last times we made love, the time you thought of hitting me, the gentle way you would stroke my back. Every touch, every not touch, catalogued in black and white.

(My father was always the one to drive me to ballet lessons, to watch, intently, with the other girls' mothers, my first stuttering attempts at the shapes of dance. Learning to stretch, point, bend until I became fluent in ballet's language, until my flesh conformed to its vocabulary. How I would see him there, out of the corner of my eye, even after his death.)

I would take Ethan to the next ballet.

I would write out this letter to you in gestures, in signs, in inkblots. Through the impoverished language of my anomia.

& & &

I would bind you like a book.

Pores like letters, the wisps of your hairs like serifs. Pages of skin, and I assemble them into signatures, like limbs. Imposition haphazard as our intentions, and I could have loved you with the resoluteness of ink. Quires of wrongs. I fold you again and again, like resentment. Collation, incontestable as bone, as longing, and I stitch the spine together, beginning to end, with a thread of anger.

I take all the pages of all the drafts of my letter to you and I press them together under this weight; from the board I cut two covers and a spine. I cover the boards with a cloth the colour of sadness and attach the endpapers, pressed from the pulp of your absence, to the beginning and the end of you.

ACKNOWLEDGEMENTS

Immense gratitude to Howard Akler for enthusiasm, compassion, and advice; to Darren Wershler-Henry for encouragement, clarity, and the ability to understand what I'm trying to say; to damian lopes for the courage to dismantle; to Stuart Ross for wisdom, steadfast faith, and a thoughtful edit; to Liz Phillips for intelligent, understanding words and an articulate paintbrush; to Lorne Bridgman for photographic miracle-working; to Andrew Currie, Jeannine MacDonald, Amanda Malitsky, and Lora Patton for their encouragement; to my mother, Katriina Alanko, and my brother, Kari Wilcox, for everything; and, of course, to Martin O'Keefe, my letter O.

Beverley Daurio is a virtuoso editor; I can't thank her enough for her perceptive reading and sharp edit. Thanks, too, to The Mercury Press for enthusiastically embarking on this project.

Thanks to the following publications in which bits of *A Grammar of Endings* (née *Anomia*), in various incarnations, have appeared: *Tessera, Quarry, Taddle Creek, Queen Street Quarterly,* and *torque.*

Quotations within the text are taken from the following: *Stedman's Medical Encyclopedia,* 25th Edition (Williams and Wilkins, 1990), *Kisses on Paper* (Jill Dawson, ed., Faber and Faber, 1994), *Love Letters* (Peter Washington, ed., Alfred A. Knopf, 1996), and *Letter Writing* (Nigel Rees, Bloomsbury, 1994).

Thanks, also, to the Canada Council for the Arts and the Toronto Arts Council for their invaluable financial assistance during the writing of this book.